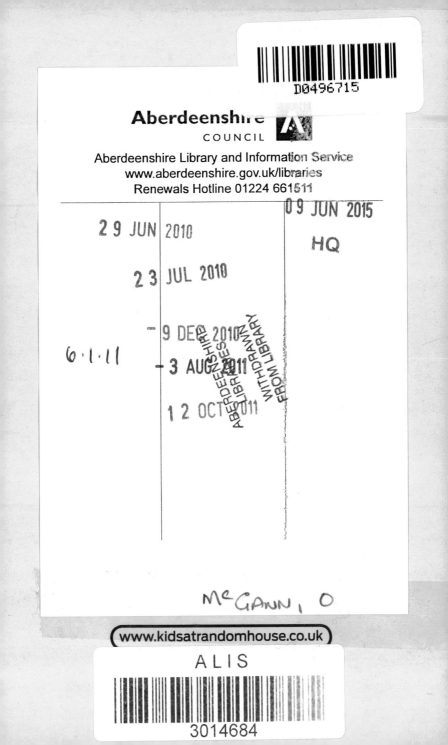

The Armouron
Don't miss any of the
titles in this awesome series:

The Armoured Ghost

Lying Eyes

The Caged Griffin

Prisoner on Kasteesh

LYING EYES

O. B. McGann

BANTAM BOOKS

ARMOURON: LYING EYES
A BANTAM BOOK 978 0 553 82117 8

First published in Great Britain by Bantam Books,
an imprint of Random House Children's Books
A Random House Group Company

Bantam edition published 2010

1 3 5 7 9 10 8 6 4 2

Mixed Sources
Product group from well-managed
forests and other controlled sources
www.fsc.org Cert no. TT-COC-2139
© 1996 Forest Stewardship Council
FSC

Set in Palatino

Bantam Books are published by Random House Children's Books,
61–63 Uxbridge Road, London W5 5SA

www.**kids**atrandomhouse.co.uk
www.**rbooks**.co.uk

Addresses for companies within The Random House Group Limited
can be found at: www.randomhouse.co.uk/offices.htm

THE RANDOM HOUSE GROUP Limited Reg. No. 954009

A CIP catalogue record for this book is available from the British Library.

Printed in the UK by CPI Bookmarque, Croydon, CR0 4TD

For centuries, an order of knights worked to keep the peace across the galaxy. Mighty warriors, the Armouron Knights fought for Honour, Duty, Compassion and Justice. They battled organized crime and helped defeat cruel dictators. They prevented wars. Life in the galaxy was not perfect, but people knew justice and peace.

Then, on one planet after another, huge corporations began to seize power. They wanted to control the entire galaxy – and only the Armouron Knights were stopping them. The corporations spread lies about the knights, turning people against them. They sent their private armies to defeat them. Terrible battles were fought but, one by one, the Armouron Knights were captured or killed.

Now the last of the Armouron are scattered around the edges of the galaxy. Not many are left, and they are getting old. A new generation is needed. Planet Earth is controlled by the Perfect Corporation. They call it a Perfect World, but in truth, it is a prison. Here, on Earth, one of the last remaining knights has recruited five young warriors to train in the ways of the Armouron. They lack experience, but they make up for it with raw talent and determination. They are the only hope for a new generation of knights.

And the galaxy needs the Armouron more than ever . . .

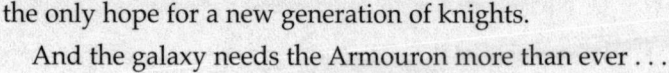

The new generation of the Armouron

Rake
Armouron title: Templer, the Fearless
Role: Strategy and Offence

Tea-Leaf
Armouron title: Balista, the Shadow
Role: Spy and Scout

Oddball
Armouron title: Sappar, the Inventive
Role: Scavenger and Engineer

Hoax
Armouron title: False-Light, the Trickster
Role: Deception and Misdirection

Snow
Armouron title: Alida, the Shieldmaiden
Role: Protection and Evasion

The Armouron master Salt

Armouron title: Claymore

Role: Master Craftsman and Teacher

The Armouron Code:

Honour, Duty, Compassion and Justice

1. Perfect Corporation
2. Gladiator Arena
3. Salt's Workshop
4. Armouron Academy
5. Old School
6. SeeBlock Tower
7. Perfect Vision HQ
8. Nu-Topia Hospital
9. Shopping Mall
10. Peace Keeps
11. Fuel Dumps
12. The Park
13. Waste Dumps
14. Epsilon Power Station
15. Spaceport

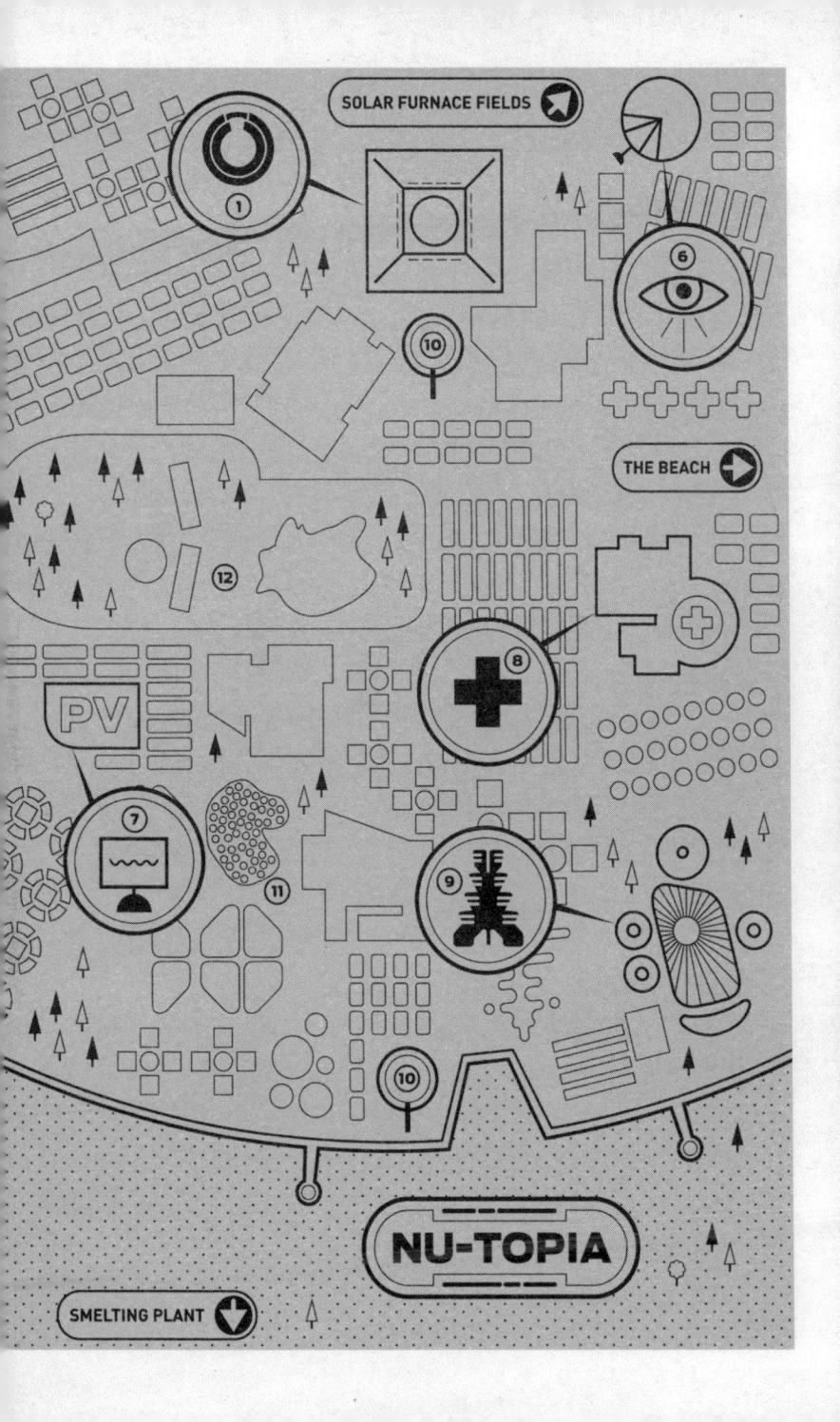

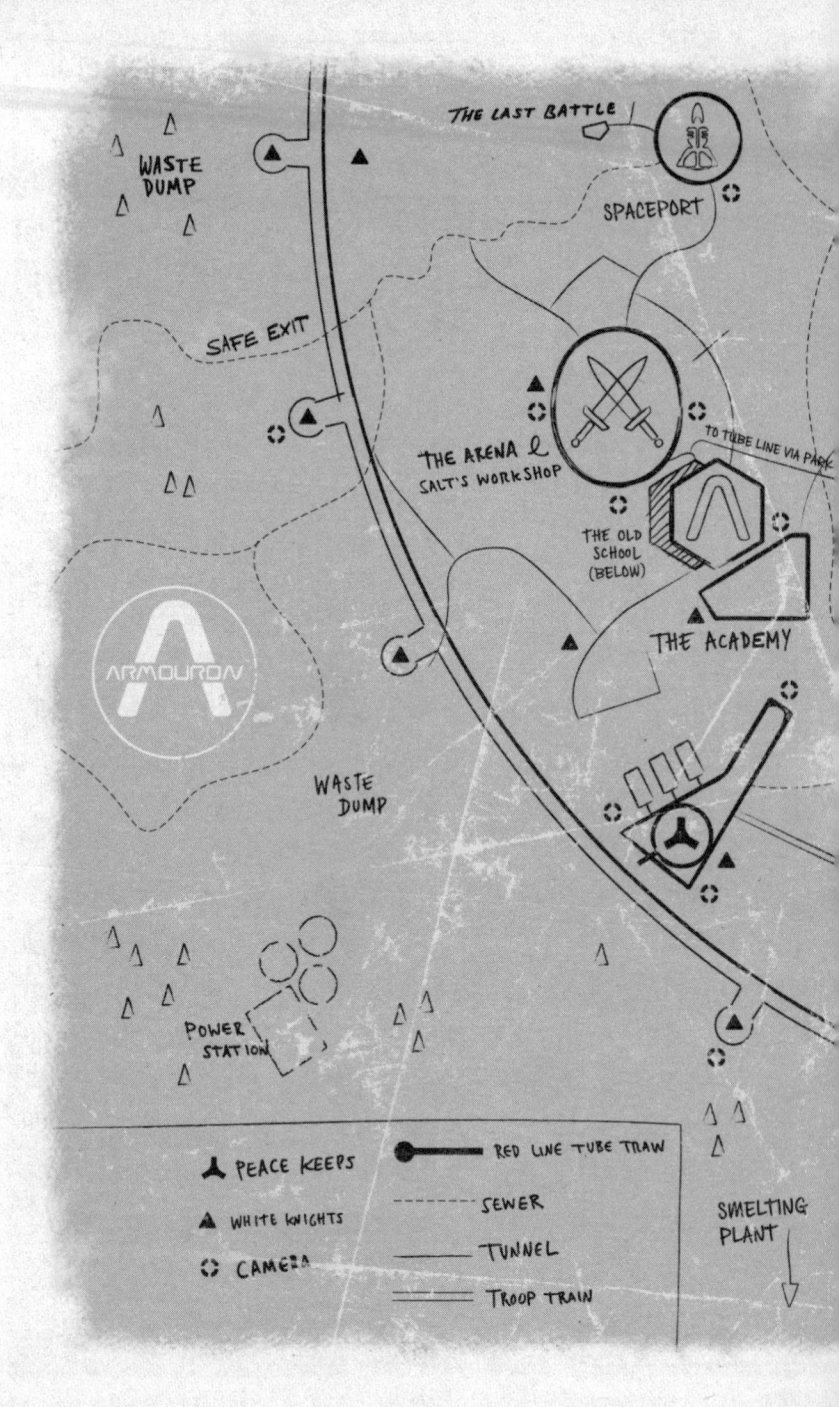

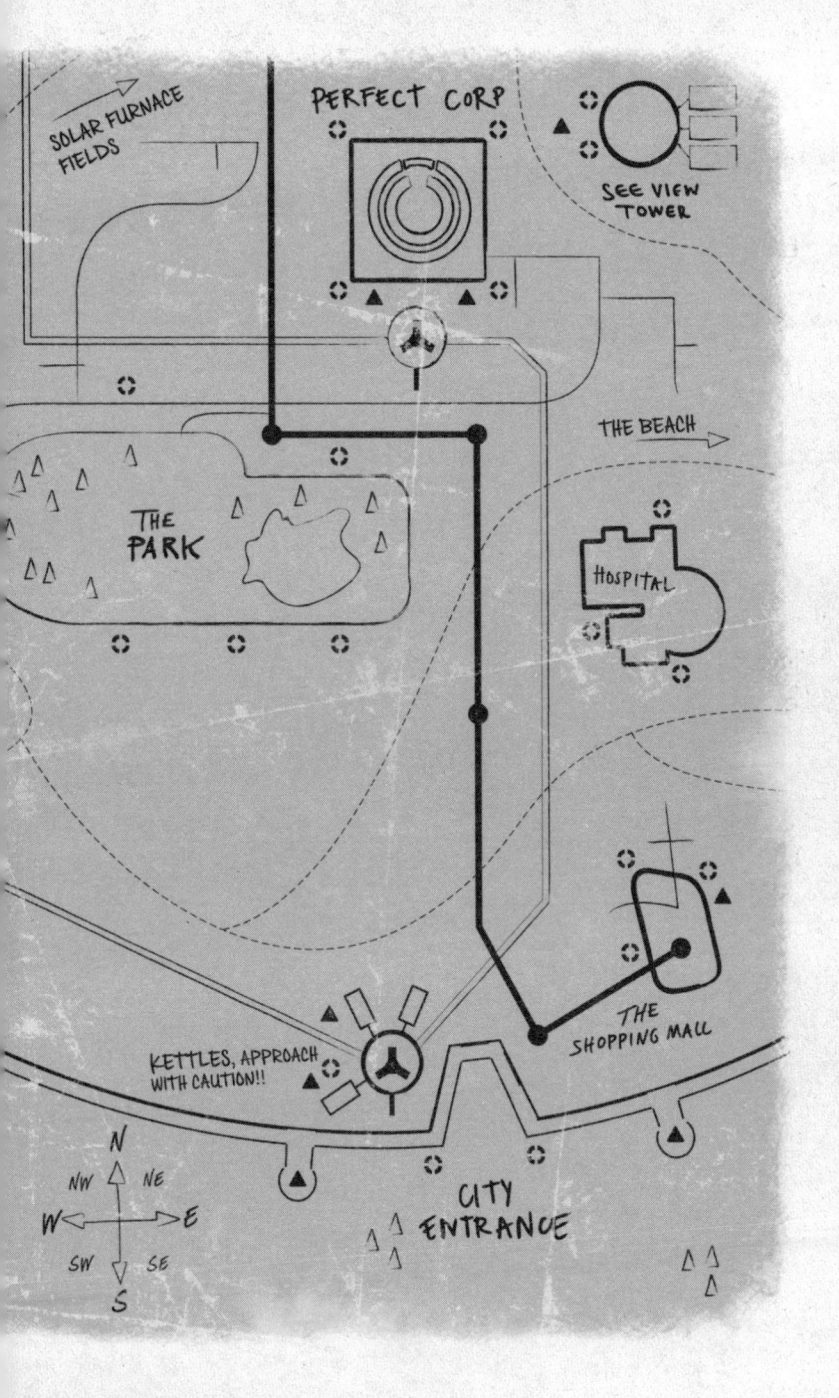

LYING EYES

Chapter 1
Across a Dark City

Keep moving, no matter what, don't stop. Rake repeated the words, over and over again, in his head as he ran. This was a race he didn't intend to lose. He was part of one team, along with Snow and Hoax. They were heading for their home, the Old School, through the dark streets of Nu-Topia.

Tea-Leaf and Oddball made up the other team. It was the middle of the night and they were all on a training exercise. Their master, Salt, had left them out in the centre of the city. Wearing their armour, they had to make their way through several kilometres of streets as fast as they could, avoiding the White Knight security patrols and the street cameras. And they had to avoid being spotted by any civilians who might also be out.

They were all still getting used to this strange, dangerous life. The gruelling training, the hiding away, the armour and weapons – these were all parts of their secret new identities as Armouron Knights. And their master had given them knights' titles to go with those identities – Templer, Alida, Sappar and False-Light. But by day, Rake, Snow, Oddball and Hoax lived a very different life.

These four lived penned up in the school known as the Academy. There, they trained to perform mock fights for the crowds who watched the Gladiator Games. It was more theatre than battle. As Armouron Knights, they had to fight for real. Nobody in the Academy knew about their secret second life, except for their master, Salt.

The four Academy cadets had been out in Nu-Topia alone before – but they had never gone this distance across the city. It was scary and exciting at the same time. The competition was all the more fierce because Rake had a point to prove.

Tea-Leaf, the fifth member of the group, had

not grown up in the Academy. The orphan, who had been given the Armouron title of Balista, had lived on the streets, raised as a survivor, rather than a fighter. As far as Rake was concerned, she had yet to earn their trust – and prove herself as a warrior.

Rake was leading his two friends along a narrow alley. He came to a corner and peered out at the street it led into. There was a camera on the top of a pole halfway down the street. He pointed two fingers towards his eyes and then pointed at the camera.

'We have to find another way round,' he whispered.

Snow and Hoax nodded. They were glad to have a rest – Rake had been running them hard. He put a hand up to his helmet and clicked a switch down. A map of this part of the city slid down in front of his eyes. His red and black helmet carried old-fashioned microfilm maps that could be viewed through his visor. The young knights couldn't use computers, phones or GPS on their missions. The Perfect Corporation, led by a creepy genius known as the Chairman, tried to control all the technology on Earth. It controlled all the electrical power in Nu-Topia, the smallest battery or power source could be detected by its satellites.

Rake found the street they were on and quickly picked out another route. This was the part that worried him. He and his fellow Academy cadets were all strangers to the city. They had to use maps to find their way around. But Tea-Leaf had grown up here; she knew the streets and the short cuts. She had an edge over them, but Rake was determined to stay ahead of her.

Oddball would slow her down a bit. He wore the heaviest armour – carried the most equipment. But he wasn't slow enough to reassure Rake.

'Back down this way,' he said softly to the others, 'and then right. We have to cut back across Tar Street and head through the park.'

Without waiting for their replies, he set off running again. Snow and Hoax looked at each other.

'"We have to cut back across Tar Street and head through the park,"' Hoax muttered in a perfect impression of Rake's determined voice. He flicked up his visor to look at Snow. 'Huh! You'd almost be tempted just to let him run off on his own, wouldn't you?'

'Yeah, except he's the one with the *maps*,' Snow replied, raising her visor to gaze back into Hoax's face.

'Good point,' he grunted. He turned and broke into a run. 'Suppose we better catch up. You know what he's like when he gets all competitive.'

Snow moved alongside Hoax, falling quiet as she kept pace with him. Her blue and grey armour was one of the lightest in the team, but like the others, she also carried a weapon in her sheath and a shield on her back. She was the youngest of the group, and didn't have the same stamina as the two older boys running with her. She was having a hard time keeping up.

'Tea-Leaf's going to win anyway,' Hoax said, 'unless we *cheat* somehow.'

'We're supposed to be Armouron Knights,' Snow reminded him. 'You know – we fight with honour?'

'Ah, I'm sure even the old Armouron pulled a few sneaky moves in their time,' he grunted.

Snapping their visors down, they caught up

with Rake, who was looking back impatiently. Leaping over walls, keeping to the shadows, darting from one piece of cover to another, they made their way towards the park that Rake had found on the map. Along the way, they had to wait twice to let White Knights go past. The tall white robot police had to be avoided at all costs. They also kept a watchful eye out for Flying Fortresses, the White Knights' air patrols. The three were all breathing hard when they reached a building site that lay by the road on one side of the park.

Creeping through the half-finished building, Hoax was first to get a view of the park. He immediately ducked back inside. With his left hand, he pulled his shield off the back of his orange and black armour. His right hand hung ready over the handles of the nunchaku in his sheath. The other two moved up beside him. They looked out through a square gap in the wall, where a window would soon be fitted. The three young knights gazed past the bars of the scaffolding outside, stunned by what they saw beyond.

Towering over the park was a giant machine. It squatted on four massive jet engines and was

covered with gun turrets. It must have been over forty metres high. Its engines alone were over half that height. They were jutting out on all four sides like legs, with the main part of the machine looming up from the centre like an armoured building.

Chapter 2
The War Machine

'What the clack is that?' Rake gasped.

'I don't know,' a voice said from above them. 'But I've never seen *anything* like this right in the middle of the city – and it's slap bang in the way of us getting home.'

Rake and the others jumped with fright, peering up into the darkness. In the rafters of the floor above them, they spotted Oddball's yellow and black armour first. But it was Tea-Leaf who had spoken, and she was harder to see. Her grey and black armour could change colour to blend into its surroundings. Rake swore under his breath. So the pair had beaten them to the park after all. Tea-Leaf and Oddball dropped quietly down to the ground.

'It doesn't look like something the Perfect Corporation owns,' Tea-Leaf added. 'They normally stick their logo all over everything. What I don't understand is how that thing can just be sitting there without anybody out looking at it. There are no guards, no lights. This should have been all over the news. If it's an alien ship, who does it belong to? Why aren't people freaking out? There should be crowds of people out there. How could it just land there without anyone causing a fuss?'

Perfect Corp controlled all the travel between Earth and other planets, but spacecraft were still a common sight in the skies. Even alien craft could be seen sometimes, but they normally landed at the city's modern spaceport. This ship was clearly not supposed to be here – and it was built for battle.

'You're right,' Snow said to Tea-Leaf, staring out at the huge war machine. 'People would panic if they saw something like this coming down out of the sky. But it's as quiet as a grave – there isn't a soul out there.'

'Maybe it's a hologram,' Hoax suggested.

'Perhaps the Chairman is testing some giant projector that just made this machine appear there. He waits until everyone goes to sleep and switches it on – just to see if he can do it.'

'It's not a hologram,' Oddball told them, tapping the front of his helmet. He always spoke a little too fast, as if his thoughts were in a constant rush. 'Our visors can see through holograms – that's one of the things *all* our suits can do, remember? The visors don't lie. Salt told us that while we have our helmets on, we can see through most illusions. We'd know if it was a hologram.'

Their suits of armour carried ancient power totems that made the young knights stronger and more agile. The suits also had other qualities, including visors that could see through illusions.

'Whatever it is, it's blocking our way home,' Snow pointed out. 'We were all supposed to go through the park. We're going to have to find a way around.'

'That's going to take ages,' Tea-Leaf said. 'There are patrols all over this part of town.'

Rake nodded.

'We can't go too far out of our way, or we

won't make it back by dawn,' he said. 'Salt will be worried about us if we're not back soon. And I don't want to be stuck out here when the sun comes up. People will be coming out on the streets. We'd be sitting ducks for the White Knights.'

'It doesn't look like it's, y'know . . . switched on,' Tea-Leaf observed. 'There are no lights on, and there's no sound coming out of it. It might just be parked up for the night. Maybe if we kept to the trees, we could sneak right past it?'

'Bad idea,' Oddball sniffed. 'We don't know what kinds of sensors that thing has. We don't even know where it's come from. I say we take the long way round.'

'Me too,' Snow said firmly. 'I've a bad feeling about this.'

Rake gazed out at the huge, dark shape against the night sky. Its guns stuck out into the dark blue like black spikes. He normally paid attention to Snow's bad feelings, but he was worried about being caught out in the city after sunrise. Apart from Tea-Leaf, they all had to be back in the Gladiator Academy before anybody noticed they were missing.

Living as Gladiator cadets by day and then

becoming Armouron Knights after darkness fell wasn't an easy existence. Sometimes Rake wished they could just give up the farce that was Gladiator training. Ever since he had learned that Gladiators were more like circus clowns than real warriors, he had really started to resent his life at the Academy. But they had to keep the Armouron team secret, so they continued with their normal lives by day. And though he would never admit it now, some small, selfish part of him still dreamed of becoming a rich and famous Gladiator.

'We have to sneak past it,' he said at last. 'We have to make it back by dawn or . . . well, we have to make it back by dawn – that's all there is to it. Come on, let's go.'

Snow and Oddball looked at each other, wanting to argue, but Tea-Leaf and Hoax were already following Rake out of the window. The decision had been made. They were going for a walk in the park.

Rake led the way, closely followed by Tea-Leaf and Hoax. Snow and Oddball followed further back. The gates into the park were locked – people were not supposed to be wandering around Nu-Topia after dark without good reason, and places like parks were normally closed up. The five knights found a spot that was sheltered by trees and jumped over the two-metre-high fence.

'I should lead,' Hoax told them. 'My father was a forest tracker – he taught me how to find my way through the woods in darkness.'

'Your father was a salesman,' Rake replied, taking the lead. 'And he taught you to tell lies and act tough when you were scared. Now, keep your eyes open. We don't know who else is in here.'

They crept through the gloom. The space under the trees was even darker, now that the light from the night sky was blocked out. They should have taken a route as far from the war machine as possible. But Rake was curious and wanted to take a closer look. If this thing was part of Perfect Corp's next big plan, Rake wanted to be able to tell their master as much as possible about it.

'Rake, don't!' Oddball called softly. 'We're getting too close!'

Rake ignored his friend, feeling more confident now that they had got this close. There was no sign of life from the huge machine. Standing under the edge of the trees, Rake could see much more of it now – the thing was only twenty metres away.

'Rake!' Tea-Leaf pulled at his arm. 'We're pushing our luck! Come on!'

He brushed her off and walked slowly out towards the nearest part of it – one of the tall engines that formed its legs. There was a gun turret on the engine itself, and many more dotted round the body of the machine. None of them were moving. Nothing about it seemed to be working.

How could it just be standing here, in the centre of a park, in the middle of the city? It was like somebody plonking a battleship in the car park of a shopping centre. Why weren't people out looking at it, pointing at it, talking about it?

He was close enough to touch it now. The thruster pod at the base of the engine was taller than he was. Reaching out, he brushed his fingers across it. The metal he felt was definitely real. Rake rapped his knuckles against it. Solid as a rock. The whole thing must have weighed hundreds of tonnes. He could see that it had sunk deep into the ground when it had landed.

Rake didn't notice that somewhere high up in

the machine, something had come alive. From inside the metal, there came a humming sound.

The metal had a strange texture, almost like a reptile's scales. Rake lifted his visor to take a closer look – and the whole enormous machine disappeared before his eyes.

Chapter 3
Ulcer

'What the—!' Rake gasped, stumbling backwards.

There was nothing but open sky above him. The machine was gone. There was a whine of machinery starting up, whirring and clanking sounds. Suddenly, Oddball was pulling him by the arm, forcing him to run back towards the trees.

'Did you see that?' Rake exclaimed. 'It just disappeared!'

'It's got a cloaking device, you idiot!' Oddball snapped at him, smacking Rake's visor back down. 'It's invisible to normal eyes. You could only see it because of your visor!'

Rake looked back. It was true – his eyes had been lying to him. The machine was visible once more, but now there were lights coming on all over it. The gun turrets were moving. And they were all pointing down at—

Rake knocked Oddball aside just as the ground they'd been on was torn apart by an explosion. Weaving right and left, they ran back to the trees as fast as their legs could carry them. Lasers punched into the ground around them. Cannon-fire pounded the stretch of grass with a line of explosions that followed the two knights into the

woods. Trees were pulverized. Fires started to spread through the woodland.

'You just couldn't leave it alone, could you?' Tea-Leaf snarled at Rake as he ran past her. She took off after him, ducking as more explosions erupted around them. 'Oh no, Mr Big-Shot has to go right up and knock on the huge doomsday machine! You bonehead!'

Rake didn't answer – he just showed her how to run faster. All five of them were fleeing through a forest fire. They reached the fence at the edge of the park and vaulted over it. In seconds, they were across the road and into a shuttle hangar on the other side, darting between the truck-sized aircraft and heading for the back entrance. Behind them, cannonfire blew up one of the vehicles and then another one. Fire mushroomed up inside the large garage, rushing along the ceiling.

The back exit was a wide emergency door, but it was locked. Oddball hit it without stopping, smashing it open. They were in an alley now, shielded from the war machine. But none of them thought that a plain old building would stop it. They kept running through the back streets, putting as much distance as possible between them and the mechanical nightmare behind them.

Back in the square around the park, lights were coming on in the buildings. People were looking out of their windows. The war machine had dropped its cloaking device to fire its weapons. Now everyone could see it. There were shouts and screams. People ran out into the streets – and then ran back into their buildings when they saw what was out there. They thought the city was under attack from an alien craft.

Then it disappeared – vanishing as if it had never been there, leaving just the damage in the park and some burning trees to prove it had ever existed at all. White Knights appeared from all sides of the square, crowding in to restore order. The people who had seen the machine would be found and questioned.

Their memories of the event would be erased.

The fire service arrived and quickly dealt with the blaze in the trees. In less than an hour, order was restored to Nu-Topia. But long before that, other things had already started happening.

Eyes that were not human were looking out from the invisible machine. An alien named Ulcer stared at the hologram screens in the control room. She looked almost human, except for her turquoise skin and large bald head. Fish-like eyes stuck out from the sides of her head, and her wide, curving mouth drooped over a sagging chin. Her skin was smooth, but mottled with spots like large freckles. Her arms and legs were thin and spindly, but still very strong.

'So much for stealth mode!' she snarled. 'What's the point in us making this thing invisible if it's programmed to shoot anything that bumps into it? That's the last time we leave this monster on automatic! You hear me, Gland?'

'Aye, aye, Captain!' her second-in-command responded.

Ulcer looked at the pictures the machine's cameras had taken as the two figures had fled into the trees. They were dressed in armour. She knew immediately that they were not Gladiators. These were Armouron Knights – the ones the Chairman had been raging about. There weren't supposed to be any left. And yet here they were.

Ulcer and her small team were spies who worked for money. Most of the time, that money came from the Perfect Corporation and its Chairman.

Designing and testing a cloaking device for this machine, the *Invader*, was just another job. Ulcer's squad were criminals on their own planet, Byel. Years before, they had been exiled for treachery. And not many Byelons managed to get exiled for that particular crime – Byel was a pretty treacherous place already.

'Ulcer!' a voice interrupted her thoughts. 'The whole point of using a *cloaking device* is that *nobody sees you*!'

A hologram of the Chairman appeared in the room beside her. He was sitting behind his huge desk. His dark hair was slicked back, making his pale skin more obvious. She looked at his pudgy figure and sighed. To think this was the most powerful man this side of the galaxy. It didn't show. But Ulcer wasn't stupid – he could order her death without a second thought.

'You and your team are supposed to be masters of *deception*!' the Chairman went on, his intelligent eyes narrowed in a cold rage. 'I hardly think blowing up a public park is a good way of hiding from sight!'

'Our cloaking device worked perfectly,' she protested, biting back her anger. 'Right up to the point where the weapons systems woke themselves up and started shooting at everything. That's not our fault – blame those trigger-happy computers!'

'Don't waste my time with excuses,' the Chairman hissed, waving his hand. 'What was the machine shooting at anyway?'

Ulcer hesitated, looking at the figures on the screens again.

'Your androids didn't see them?' she asked.

'No.'

'We didn't get a good look at them either,' she told him. 'I think they were just some kids sneaking into the park. Probably bumped into us by mistake and got the fright of their lives.'

'Well it's an almighty mess to clear up because of some nosey kids,' snapped the Chairman. 'You only had to stay there one night to test the cloak. See if you can finish the job without blowing up anything else.'

The hologram shimmered and disappeared.

Ulcer smiled. Perhaps this was a good thing after all. The White Knights had not arrived in time to spot the knights. This was excellent. She wanted them for herself. The Chairman would pay a high price for such hated enemies.

'Gland!' she barked.

'Aye, Captain?' her lieutenant replied from behind her, giving her a salute.

'Send the squad out into the streets.' Ulcer stood up from her seat, still looking at the screens. 'We're going to find these knights ourselves. I'll be going out too. Don't alert the White Knights – at least not yet. You stay here and secure the Invader. Be ready if we call you for back-up.'

'Aye, Captain, I'll keep her ship-shape, primed and ready,' came the reply, as the lieutenant took the commander's seat.

'Oh, and Gland?' Ulcer said, as she headed for the door.

'Aye, Captain?'

'Stop calling me "captain". Ever since we were hired to stick a cloaking shield on this crate, you've been acting like some kind of cartoon pirate. Keep at it and I'll take us up to twenty thousand metres and make you walk the plank. Got it?'

'Aye, Cap— I mean . . . Right. Sorry, Ulcer.'

Ulcer took the elevator down towards the bottom hatch to join her hunting team of five Byelons. As she glided down the shaft, her skin became covered in spots that swelled and grew until they covered the entire surface of her body. When they all joined up, she was a different colour, a slightly different shape. She looked human. The five members of her squad had also adopted human shapes. This was why Byelons were mistrusted across the galaxy. They were shape-changers – and Ulcer's group were expert assassins.

Ulcer examined their disguises and nodded her approval. She waved her hand at a control panel and the hatch slid open.

'Bring me the Armouron warriors,' she said. 'Alive, if possible. If not – dead will do just fine.'

Then the six agile figures raced out into the night.

Chapter 4
Hanging Out at the Mall

The five Armouron Knights ducked behind a parked truck, crouching down in the shadow of a stack of crates to catch their breath. They had been running for half an hour. Three times, they had almost been spotted by White Knight patrols. Once, they had been forced to take cover as a heavily armed Flying Fortress passed overhead.

'How could you be that stupid?' Tea-Leaf hissed at Rake, opening her visor so he could see the anger on her face.

'I'm sorry, all right?' he sniped back at her. 'I just wanted to get a closer look.'

'Any closer and we'd have been cooked in our shells like turtles,' Oddball snorted.

'Normally, having guns all over something is a way of saying "Go away",' Snow pointed out. 'People could have been hurt, Rake. And I don't just mean us. Normal people.'

'But us too,' Hoax reminded her.

'I'm *sorry*!' Rake shouted. 'I screwed up, OK? I won't do it again. Now, if you're done, can we see about getting home before anything else happens? Tea-Leaf, do you know where we are?'

'Yeah,' she replied. 'We've been heading in the right direction, but we've still got a long way to go. And now there's this massive shopping mall in our way, just down this street. It's too big to go round – we have to go through.'

'No way! You said the same thing about the *park*,' Hoax told her. 'I think we should just keep going *round* stuff from now on. Who knows, there could be a nuclear submarine or something parked in there. I heard somewhere that a lot of the malls in Nu-Topia are guarded by swarms of specially trained killer wasps at night.'

They were all well used to Hoax's wild imagination, so nobody bothered to say anything. Rake was looking at the map overlaid on his visor. He clicked it back up again and looked at Hoax.

'She's right, we can't go round,' he said. 'This place is massive. There are car parks on either side of it too, and they're each nearly a kilometre wide. And they'll have cameras on them. But there's bound to be cameras inside too, Tea-Leaf. What do we do about those?'

'I can take some of them out with my crossbow,' she told him. 'Look, the White Knights have got to be searching for us by now anyway. We need to move fast – we have to take the risk. If we can get to the other side without being spotted, we might be able to hitch a ride on one of the underground trains. The Red Line runs right under the shopping mall and it could take us most of the way home.'

'Let's do it,' Oddball said.

The others nodded. As one group, they left their hiding place and made their way down the street. At the end of this street lay another one at right angles to it. The shopping mall loomed over them. The car parks for the mall lay on either side of it, but the knights couldn't see them from where they stood. The buildings were curving, glittering blocks of steel and glass. They stretched off down the street in either direction.

'Wow,' Hoax said, whistling.

'Told you we weren't going round it,' Tea-Leaf said.

She didn't go up to the main doors. Instead, she led them down the street a bit and found a grate in the pavement. It was locked, but she took a pick from a slot in her gauntlet and had the lock open in seconds. The grate opened on hinges and they all climbed down into the darkness beneath. Tea-Leaf closed the grate after them and locked it.

They were in a low concrete tunnel. Large bunches of cables snaked along the ceiling and the walls were bare of paint. It was the type of passageway that often ran under large buildings. Filled with electrical cabling and plumbing, it kept workmen out of the way of the customers.

'This only goes in the right direction for a while,' Tea-Leaf told them. 'Then we need to go through the shopping levels.'

They followed the tunnel for about a hundred metres. Their visors made it easier to see in the dark, but it was still a dull, gloomy place. At the end of the tunnel there was a branch and a door just round the corner. Tea-Leaf picked this lock as well, and they went through. They climbed a couple of flights of stairs and came out into a much nicer tunnel. It was a corridor with painted walls and a polished floor. Advertisements for all sorts of products flickered across screens on the walls.

'Why are these switched on?' Snow asked, pointing at the screens. 'Who are they advertising this stuff to? Nobody's here.'

'I don't think they can be switched off,' Oddball said.

'Keep your eyes open for cameras,' Rake muttered. 'This place is going to be littered with them.'

Tea-Leaf took her crossbow from its sheath, crept to the end of the tunnel and peered out. She took aim at something and fired. There was a *crack* as something broke further out.

'That's one down,' she said. 'At least we can get out of this corridor. But I can't shoot all of them. You guys are going to have to get good at sneaking.'

The concourse was a huge space surrounded by shops. There were a dozen areas like it in the shopping mall. Elevators and escalators linked the different floors to one another. Plants and small trees grew out of large pots. The five knights walked past shops selling everything from clothes to pets, electronics to cosmetics. There were screens showing eye-catching ads on every wall and in every window. Holograms even floated in the air, advertising a wide range of products. The knights had to actually walk through some of them.

Sometimes, Tea-Leaf had to shoot down another camera, but most of the time, they were able to creep past them. Eventually, they came to the central concourse, a massive open space the size of a football field. A glass ceiling with steel ribs stretched overhead.

Like the rest of the place, it was dimly lit, with only every third or fourth light switched on. There were seats and tables here, where people could sit out under the glass and plan the next stages of their shopping expeditions. Scattered around them were ad banners and potted plants and trees. There were even a few fountains. Tea-Leaf led the knights down one side, along the windows of a large electronics store.

'There's a blind spot here, where the cameras can't see,' she told them. 'I think we can get all the way down the length of the concourse just by staying on this side.'

No sooner had she said the words than Snow held up her hand in a warning gesture. She tapped her ear and pointed down the concourse. She could hear someone coming.

Looking around quickly, they searched for somewhere to hide. They were trapped between the shop on one side and the open space covered by the cameras on the other.

'For clack's sake, just *hide*!' Rake hissed at them. 'Anywhere you can!'

He ducked into the shadow of an escalator. Oddball stepped behind a tall banner screen advertising a treatment for head-lice. Snow climbed up a pillar and hung in the shadows under a footbridge crossing the concourse, and Hoax crept behind a large bush planted in a wooden barrel.

Tea-Leaf waited until the last second, listening to the footsteps approaching, trying to figure out where they were coming from. There was the sound of chanting now. She stepped back into a doorway and her suit darkened to match the shadows around her.

Moments later, a group of figures came out of

a corridor further down. They too were keeping in to the side of the concourse, as if they knew the cameras could not see them there. They were going to walk right past the Armouron Knights.

Rake was nearest to them. His eyes widened as they drew closer and he got a better look. There were at least fifteen or sixteen of them. Dressed in long grey cloaks, they walked with a kind of slinky movement, their heads down, weaving from side to side. They chanted quietly as they walked. Under the hoods of their cloaks, he was shocked to see what he thought were cat-like faces, until he realized they were all wearing masks.

Each figure also carried a cat on their shoulder, or sometimes even on their head. From time to time as they moved, one of them would give out a hushed 'miaow' or purr as they brushed up against each other.

'Aw, you've gotta be kidding me,' Rake murmured under his breath.

One of the cats, a stocky ginger tom, jumped down off its owner's shoulder and started sniffing around. It hopped up on the barrel of the bush Hoax was standing behind. Digging a little hole, it squatted and relieved itself before burying the results. Then it made its way round the bush, looked up at Hoax, and started mewing.

Hoax tried to brush it away, but it began pawing at him.

'Shoo!' he whispered. 'Go on! Go away!'

Its owner stopped and looked over, trying to catch sight of the cat. The group came to a sudden halt too, waiting to see what was wrong. Rake swore under his breath and gripped the handle of his sword. The owner of the ginger cat came forward, moving as if he was trying to copy the way a cat stalked its prey. The figure in the cloak looked behind the bush.

Hoax tried to move further away. But the plant just wasn't that big. He ended up sliding into view on the other side, where all the others could see him. He stood there, fidgeting, not sure what to do. For once, he didn't have a lie ready to explain his situation.

The owner of the cat spun round to his gang and let out a loud yowl. The cats jumped down from their owners' shoulders and started hissing. The gang of cat-lovers snarled and crouched down, ready to pounce, their hands curled into claws. Rake leaped out, leaving his sword in its sheath, but able to draw it at any moment. Around him, the other knights appeared, standing ready.

Chapter 5
Catfight

The five Armouron Knights did not draw their weapons or shields. The cat gang did not seem to be armed. The two sides stared at each other, each waiting for their opponents to make the first move.

'Who are you?' Rake asked.

'No – who are *you*?' the ginger cat owner replied.

They could tell from his voice that he was a man, but he still tried to sound like a cat. His mask was ginger, like his cat. All the cats' owners had masks that matched their pets.

'Oh, come on, look . . . we asked you first,' Rake said.

'But *this* is *our* territory,' the cat man replied. 'We will tolerate no rivals on our turf.'

His cat glided over to Snow, curling round her legs and purring. She gave a little sigh and picked it up, stroking it. It looked up at her and mewed happily.

'We're not trying to take over your territory,' she said in a calm voice. 'We're Armouron Knights. You've nothing to fear from us. We're not looking for any trouble.'

'Well, you've *found* trouble,' the cat man replied. 'And it's *you* who has reason to fear. Put my cat down. Tyrannosaur! Bad cat! Come here, boy! Come here!' Tyrannosaur the cat dropped out of Snow's hands and slinked reluctantly back to its master. The man pointed at the knights again. 'As for you lot . . . you claim to be Armouron? A sad joke. The Armouron are dead and gone. We are the Cat People. By day, we pretend to be *normal*. But it is just an *act*. In reality, we live our lives by the *Way of the Cat*. We are the Cat People. We rule the night.'

'Right,' said Rake, holding up his hands. 'You can have the night all to yourselves once we get out of here. But right now we're tired, we're

🟦 🟡 🔺 ⚫ 🔷 🅰 🔄 🟢 ⬡

hungry and we've still got a long way to go to get home. And frankly, it's hard to take you seriously with this whole . . . y'know, cat thing you've got going on. That's OK, though, that's cool. If you'll just move out of our way, we'll be heading off.'

Snow rolled her eyes. Rake could be a bit too blunt sometimes. She was feeling uneasy about this. These people weren't working for the Perfect Corporation – they were just a gang of weirdos who liked to dress up. The knights should be avoiding a fight if they could. But the way the Cat People were gathering around them, making hissing and snarling noises didn't sound too good.

Snow's instincts were telling her this whole thing was a distraction from the real threat. There was a much greater danger close at hand – and she was learning to trust her instincts. Rake didn't sense the same threat, but he was getting impatient anyway. He made to walk past the gang, but they shifted to block his way.

'You,' said the Cat People's leader, pointing at Rake, and then at all the knights. 'You must pay us. If you want to pass, you must pay for *safe passage*.'

'*Ah, japes,*' Tea-Leaf sighed. 'Look, I get that this place is your turf, but all we want is to get off it, OK? This city is our home too . . .'

She started walking right through the gang of Cat People. As one, they pounced on her. With yowls and screeches, they hit and kicked her and tore at her armour with their bare hands.

Rake swore to himself. The petty part of him was tempted to leave Tea-Leaf to sort it out herself. But the feeling only lasted an instant. He looked at his team-mates.

'Stand Together!' he called out.

'Battle as One!' they barked.

They leaped into the fight. There were three times as many Cat People as there were knights. But the kids had their armour – which also enhanced their strength and skill – and they trained under one of the finest warriors in the galaxy. Even so, the Cat People proved they were not going to be easy to beat. They were quick and agile. The knights' martial arts skills were only just enough to handle the weird gang.

Rake blocked two punches from one cloaked figure, kicked the guy's legs out from under him and spun to kick another one in the stomach,

pitching her into a cluster of potted plants. A punch from a third cat man just bounced off his helmet. He dragged a fourth attacker off Oddball, who punched two more. Oddball leaped into the air and kicked out at a guy who was jumping towards him. The two of them clashed in mid-air. Oddball's foot connected with the guy's chest and knocked him into a fountain.

The cat man landed in a cluster of his friends, who were still trying to get their hands on

Tea-Leaf. She used her fists and elbows to make some room and then swung her foot up and round, catching two of them across their heads. Then Hoax was there, hurling an opponent over his shoulder and sweeping the legs out from under another one. He ducked a strike and dealt out a few more punches.

'Japes!' he exclaimed, turning towards Snow. 'It's like fighting a gang of rubber bands!'

He was about to get jumped from behind, but Snow saved him, seizing the attacker's arm and flipping him onto his back. Dodging a roundhouse kick, she dropped to the floor herself and spun round, her legs stretched out wide, sweeping two more of them off their feet. They hit out at her as they fell, but their strikes were deflected by her armour. A fourth one came at her, but Rake was there, blocking the blow long enough for her to butt the guy in the stomach with her helmet.

The Cat People were lying all over the ground, groaning and rubbing their injuries. Some were comforted by their cats – others weren't. The knights stood over them, waiting for another attack, but it didn't come. Hoax sniffed.

'The Cat People *rule the night*,' he whined,

imitating Ginger's voice. 'Rule the night, my big fat—'

'We should get out of here,' Snow urged her friends, looking up through the glass at the sky, without being sure why. 'The noise might have attracted attention.'

They all nodded and started to go on their way.

'Hold on,' Hoax said, gazing down at their beaten opponents in their strange outfits. 'I'm thinking we need a new look for our night out in the city.'

Rake looked at him, and then down at the Cat People.

'Yeah,' he agreed, nodding. 'And I think *they* need to pay a charge – for safe passage.'

A couple of minutes later, all the Cat People had been stripped of their clothes, cloaks and masks. They stood there in their underwear, glaring hatefully at the knights. Careful not to let their faces be seen, the five kids took off their helmets. They each pulled on a mask and covered their suit of armour with a cloak.

They would take the rest of the Cat People's clothes with them – to make sure the cat gang didn't try to follow them. Now, at least if the five kids were seen, they wouldn't look like Armouron Knights.

'Thanks, we owe you one,' Oddball said to the Cat People with a smile in his voice.

'You won't get away with this!' the ginger cat man hissed.

'Wow – never thought I'd hear *that* line for real,' Tea-Leaf remarked from behind her tabby cat mask. 'Although . . . it's hard to take seriously, coming from someone who's dressed in nothing but their underwear.'

'Come on, guys,' Rake said to the rest of the team. 'We've got some distance to cover. Let's get moving.'

And with that, they were gone, sprinting down the side of the concourse with their cloaks trailing behind them. They dumped the rest of the Cat People's clothes in a bin as soon as they were out of sight.

Tea-Leaf led the team to a flight of stairs. The closest way out was three levels up. They passed through a food-court where a range of eating places sold fast food. The food-court looked out on the concourse below. Tea-Leaf led her friends down a corridor that led to an emergency exit. Before following them, Snow slipped past the rows of lightweight furniture to the rail and looked out over the concourse.

She was getting one of her feelings again. Something about the way the ginger cat man had looked at them told her that this wasn't over. There was a terrible anger in him. And he wasn't the type to quit. Snow sensed that the knights had got off easy this time. Turning round, she followed the others down the corridor.

Back out in the concourse, the Cat People all looked at each other, trying to hide their humiliation. Some of the underwear they had on was a bit embarrassing too.

'What do we do now?' one of the women asked her leader.

Ginger rubbed some warmth into his bare arms and scowled as he looked around at his followers. His cat wound in and out between his ankles.

'First, we get some more clothes,' he growled. 'Then we round up all the other cat-folk and get some weapons too. Then we go after those kids. Let's see how tough they are when there's twice as many of us. Their fancy armour and their flash tricks won't save them then. I bet they're dog-lovers too, those little brats. Send out the word. Gather the others. It's night-time, my people. Time to hunt!'

Chapter 6
Taking the Train

The cloaks the knights wore were too long. Most of the Cat People were adults and the knights were still kids. It had been hard to find cloaks that were the right length, but would still fit over their armour. So they dragged along the ground a little. The emergency exit that Tea-Leaf found led out onto a roof.

They could see a lot of the city from here – shuttles glided across the sky and vehicles drew lines of light along the multi-lane roads. Even out here, the young knights could see ads flashing across the sides of buildings, huge towers that reached into the clouds. The knights climbed down a ladder to the car park.

'There's an entrance to the station, just over there.' Tea-Leaf pointed, indicating a sign attached to some railings. It was for a train station, and the railings curved around the top of a ramp that led underground. 'The trains on this line start running about now, getting ready for the morning rush hour. I've ridden on the roofs a few times, but sometimes you can sneak inside. We might be able to manage it in these outfits. Could get some funny looks, but this line will get us most of the way home.'

'Let's chance it,' Rake said. 'There must be a lot of freaks wandering around at this time of the morning.'

'Actually, you don't get many freaks out in the open in Nu-Topia,' Tea-Leaf said, as she walked towards the ramp. 'They're not really allowed. The White Knights give them a hard time.'

Snow lifted her cat mask, pulled back her hood and opened her cloak to look down at the lightweight blue and grey armour covering her body.

'Wait till they get a look at us,' she said.

Down at the bottom of the ramp, the station's escalators were already working. The knights rode them down into the station. There were automatic barriers blocking the way in. They could force their way through, but it would set off the alarms. They had to buy tickets. And you needed an identity disc to get a ticket. Rake, Snow, Oddball and Hoax had them in the Academy, but they never took them out on a mission. Tea-Leaf didn't have one at all. She lived as a criminal, in the world under the city. The discs could be tracked by Perfect Corp and detected by the White Knights.

Oddball grinned and rubbed his hands together. He crouched down in front of a ticket machine, taking some tools from a compartment in his armour.

'Don't make it explode,' Rake said to him.

'The only machines I blow up are the ones I *want* to blow up,' Oddball retorted.

He opened up a panel and fiddled around with the electronics inside. A minute later, the machine spat five tickets into the dispenser.

'Nice one,' Tea-Leaf said.

'You should see what I can do with a microwave oven,' he replied.

After they were through the barriers, they all

stood around the hologram map projected from an info-stand and argued about which line it was best to take. There were three going in the right direction, but none of them went all the way to the Academy.

Eventually, they settled on one and made their way down to the platform. The lights were on in the station. Thankfully, there was no one in sight. There were cameras around though. And five kids walking around in cloaks and cat masks to cover their suits of armour couldn't help but feel a bit odd. Seeing each other in the bright light was even stranger than walking around in the dark city.

'It's like something you'd see on Halloween,' Tea-Leaf muttered.

'What's Halloween?' the others all asked at the same time.

'Japes, don't they let you have any fun in the Academy?' she exclaimed. 'You know – Halloween! You dress up, go round houses doing trick-or-treat . . .'

Her voice trailed off as she saw the blank looks on the faces of the Academy cadets. Shaking her head in pity, she was about to explain further when they heard the sound of a train coming down the tunnel. They all watched nervously. There was no telling if the sight of these cloaked figures would cause alarm – and once they were on the train, it would be much harder to escape.

The sleek metal and glass tube slid into the station, gliding to a stop at the platform. A set of doors opened right in front of the knights. They looked at one another for a moment . . . and then stepped inside.

Nobody else was on board. No alarms went off. There was nothing but the quiet hum of the train's motors, the beeping of the doors and the 'shuuush-klunk' as they closed. The train started moving. Looking around, they found themselves in a clean, modern train carriage. Square bays, each with four seats, ran down each side of the compartment. Not knowing what else to do, the five knights picked a seat each and sat down. It all felt a bit strange.

'Do you think we should leave the masks on?' Snow asked.

And then the door opened at the end of the carriage and two White Knights walked in.

Chapter 7
The Kettles

Most people in Nu-Topia believed that the White Knights were humans in armour, like the Armouron Knights who commanded the police forces in the old days. In fact, the White Knights – or 'Kettles', as the Armouron called them – were androids. Intelligent robots, linked to satellites, the android police patrolled the city and kept order. And they kept its people completely under the control of the Perfect Corporation.

The two white figures strode down the carriage towards the five new passengers. Rake made sure the handle of his sword was easy to reach under his cloak. He flicked his eyes towards the others, and saw they were all ready to move. But there were cameras in the carriage, and the White Knights could send warnings out by satellite link. A fight now could bring the whole police force down on them – and trapped in this train, they had nowhere to go.

The White Knights stopped in front of the group. Each of the robots was armed with a sword, an unfolding shield and a stun-gun. The two tall white androids looked down at the five figures in cloaks and cat masks. There was a long, tense moment of silence. Then one of the robots spoke:

'Good morning, citizens. Tickets please.'

The five knights, who had been preparing themselves to leap into action, were forced to fumble around for their tickets instead. Taking them from the pockets inside their cloaks, they each handed up their card. The robot scanned them and handed them back. Then it looked down at Hoax.

'Please remove your mask, citizen. And show me your identity disc.'

Hoax hesitated for a moment. He didn't have a disc. And his identity was on file at the Academy. If the robot saw his face, it would know he was not supposed to be here. If he didn't show his face, the android police would arrest them anyway.

But his hesitation was enough for the White Knight. Citizens of Nu-Topia never failed to obey commands from the police. The robots' hands went to their stun-guns. Any second now, they would be signalling an arrest to the communication satellites.

The edge of the blade of Rake's sword was as thin as an atom. It could easily cut through the hardened plastic of the robot's armour. As the first White Knight went to draw its stun-gun, Rake's blade cut off the top of the robot's head.

The crown of the armoured head tumbled to the ground, the android's skull spat sparks and let out a broken whirring sound. The second White Knight barely had time to see Rake move before Snow swung the edge of her shield out and up, cutting its head from its neck. The head bounced off the window, cracking the glass. The two heavy mechanical bodies crumpled to the floor at almost the same time.

'Do you think they got a signal out?' Hoax asked.

Oddball crouched down beside the android that

was missing the top of its head. He pulled a cable from his gauntlet, disconnected something in the skull and inserted the end of his cable instead. The knights could not carry power sources, like batteries or generators, with them. But Oddball and Tea-Leaf could both tap into computers.

Oddball opened up a small screen in his gauntlet, using the White Knight's energy core to power it. A string of code scrolled down the screen.

'They managed to get an alert out, telling the satellites where we are,' he told them, as he disconnected again. 'But no images were sent.'

'It won't take them long to check the train cameras though,' Snow added, pointing at the

✾ ☷ ⬢ ☉ ◉ ⓐ ⬥ ⬠ ◎ ✦

little plastic dome at the end of the carriage.

'So there's more coming,' Rake grunted. 'But they don't know what we look like yet. Well, that's something. But we have to get off this train before the next stop.'

'That won't be easy,' Tea-Leaf told him. 'It's moving at over a hundred kilometres an hour. Not all the stations are open yet, so it can go faster. But it's bound to stop somewhere in the next couple of minutes.'

Rake took his shield off his back and used it to smash out the rest of the window broken by the other robot's head.

'We need to get out on the roof before this train stops and those doors open,' he said. 'Masks and cloaks off – helmets on. We can bring the disguises with us, but the cloaks could catch on something if we wore them out there. Come on, move!'

Outside, the wind blowing past the fast-moving train hit them like a hurricane. There was only a narrow gap between the train and the tunnel, so they had to keep their bodies pressed against the body of the train as they clambered up onto the roof. Up on top, the roof of the tunnel whisked past above them. Pipes and cable runs stuck out from the ceiling, threatening to knock them off the train.

They clung onto the ribbed roof of the train with fingertips and toes. It raced through the tunnel, swerving along the curving track, the dim lights rushing past them.

'Now what?' Oddball shouted over the noise of the wind.

'We wait for it to slow down enough for us to jump off!' Rake called back.

'That's *it*? You got us out here for *that*? Not much of a plan!' Tea-Leaf yelled.

'It's the best I've got right now!'

Just at that moment, the train approached a junction. There was another train waiting there for it to pass. The tunnel widened. The roof was higher here. The knights' train slowed down as it passed alongside the other one. Rake waved to the others and rose into a crouching position.

'Now!' he roared, and jumped.

With cries of frightened desperation, the others got up and leaped off the moving train. They were still moving fast, and the roof of the second train wasn't moving at all. They scraped and bumped and tumbled across it – Rake just managed to stop himself falling over the far side. He was scrabbling back on when Oddball slid right into him. Rake fell backwards, but Oddball managed to grab him. Rake was able to get hold of the edge, brace his feet against the side and vault back onto the top. The rest of them had made it safely, scattered along the roof of the train.

They all lay flat on the ribbed metal, trembling. The train they had just left carried on down the track, disappearing into the darkness of the tunnel. They waited for their hearts to start pounding.

'I'm never doing that again!' Snow protested.

With the junction clear, their new train started off again. It was going back in the direction they had just come.

'Oh, great,' Hoax groaned. 'We're going to end up right back where we started.'

'If we're lucky,' Tea-Leaf replied. 'This line goes all the way to the far side of the city. We could end up further away than when we started. Nice one, Rake.'

'Salt must be going out of his mind by now,' Snow sighed.

'I keep thinking about those three rules Salt's always drilling into us,' Rake said to them, hugging the roof of the train. 'You know, the ones you should never break when you're fighting an enemy that controls your land: Stay out of sight. Stay friends with the local people. Stay out of places where you could get cornered. You don't break those rules if you want to stay alive.'

For a minute, they all brooded on the events of the night, as the train hurtled ever further down the dark tunnel.

'Maybe we shouldn't be in such a hurry to get home,' Oddball commented. 'The way things have gone, even if we do get back, Salt's liable to kill us himself.'

Chapter 8
Dressed as Dracula

They broke another window to get inside the train. When it stopped at the station they had just escaped from, they already had their masks and cloaks back on. The doors beeped and slid open.

'If somebody's watching through the station cameras,' Hoax commented, as they stepped onto the platform, 'they're going to think there's no one but Cat People travelling on the trains this morning.'

With an alert of trouble on the trains, they couldn't take the chance of trying to get on another one. They would have to find a different way home. Heading up the tunnel towards the exit, they pushed out through the barriers. Suddenly, they heard the sounds of shouting and running feet ahead. A woman came sprinting round the corner with a gang of young men and women hot on her heels. At first, the knights thought this must be the Cat People again, but they were dressed differently.

Each one was wearing the same kind of outfit, even the women: a black suit, white shirt and waistcoat, a red cravat and a black cloak with a red lining. Each gang member had black hair and large fangs in their mouth. They shrieked and laughed as they chased after the woman. There must have been nearly twenty of them.

'I've seen those kinds of clothes before, but I can't figure out where,' Rake thought out loud.

'Old movies,' Hoax told him. 'They're all dressed as Dracula – they're pretending to be vampires.'

'Never a dull moment, is there?' Snow muttered.

'All right, let's sort this out,' Rake growled.

'Don't get us involved in this,' Tea-Leaf warned him. 'We need to get out of here. We don't have time to get into another fight.'

'The woman's in trouble,' Rake said, turning to

stare at her. 'We're Armouron Knights – or *some of us* are, at least. This is what we do.'

'Right, so do we keep the cat masks on or not?' Tea-Leaf sniffed.

'Eh . . . well, they're almost here now,' he replied, waving his hand at the gang. 'We'd better just stay dressed like this, I suppose.'

The woman skidded to a stop when she saw the figures in the Cat People outfits. Looking back at the vampire gang, she glanced warily at the knights. The gang slowed down as they realized what was ahead.

'It's all right, ma'am,' Rake said, trying to disguise his voice by making it deeper. 'We'll protect you.'

'Yes,' Hoax added, imitating Rake's fake voice. 'The Cat People will save you!'

The other knights turned to look at him for a moment, but then went back to facing the opposing gang.

'I was just on my way home . . . from my mother's,' the woman told them. 'And these maniacs tried to attack me. They're out of their minds.'

The gang's victim was a pretty young woman,

about medium height, with long brown hair tied into a pony-tail. She was dressed in the clothes of a typical Nu-Topian citizen. Her loose white trousers and green tunic had the usual Perfect Corp brands on them.

'We're not insane,' one of the gang snarled, stepping forward. 'Once darkness falls, the world belongs to us. We're the Vampires. We rule the night.'

'Here we go again,' Oddball said under his breath.

'No,' Hoax called to the Vampires. 'The *Cat People* rule the night!'

'Will you shut up?' Rake whispered.

'I'm just acting the part,' Hoax replied, tapping his mask.

'Well, *stop*,' Rake said through his teeth.

'This is the land of darkness – *our* land!' the lead Vampire snapped, baring his long fangs. The Cat People didn't seem to be paying enough attention to him. 'There's less than three hours until dawn. Until first light, nobody comes here without our say-so! Empty your pockets! Get your wallets out. We're taking all your valuables. If you're lucky, you might live to see the sunrise.'

'Are those *real* fangs?' Snow asked. 'I mean, you're not really vampires, are you? Why do you get all dressed up like that?'

'Look who's talking, Kitty-Cat!' the Vampire leader growled. 'Now, pay up or there's going to be trouble!'

For a moment, the five kids didn't reply. Then they spread out slightly and raised their hands in a fighting stance.

'It's been that kind of night,' Rake sighed.

The Vampires attacked. They fought using some weird kung fu style and their long fangs. The knights' helmets were hanging from the hips of their armour suits, under their cloaks. With their heads and necks unprotected, the young warriors had to take care not to let the weirdos bite them.

The first one came at Tea-Leaf, who knocked away his hands, grabbed him by the collar of his cloak and let herself fall backwards, using her foot to flip him over her head. He flew through the air and smashed through the window of a ticket booth behind her. She was on her feet before two more could kick out at her, deflecting them both, punching one and kicking the other in the chest.

Hoax leaped into the air, jumping off the

shoulders of one Vampire, kicking another in the head and landing on a third, knocking him out. His first opponent got back up, only to be hit on the head with Hoax's helmet, which the knight swung up from under his cloak.

Rake found himself buried under four of them. He butted one in the stomach and thumped another in the ribs. He swept the foot from under the third one, kicking the woman away as she stumbled. Grabbing the arm of the last one, he swung him round, twisted his wrist and threw him into an ad-screen that was trying to sell perfume.

Snow had her shield out, blocking a hail of fists and feet from the Vampires attacking her. She smacked the flat of the shield across one head, whacked it back against another face and slammed the edge of it into a third man's shin, making him howl. Another Vampire came at her and she caught him with a roundhouse kick, knocking out his false vampire's teeth.

Her shield was grabbed by yet another gang member, who held onto it and shoved her up against a railing. One of his friends came up on the other side of the rail. This one carried a dagger.

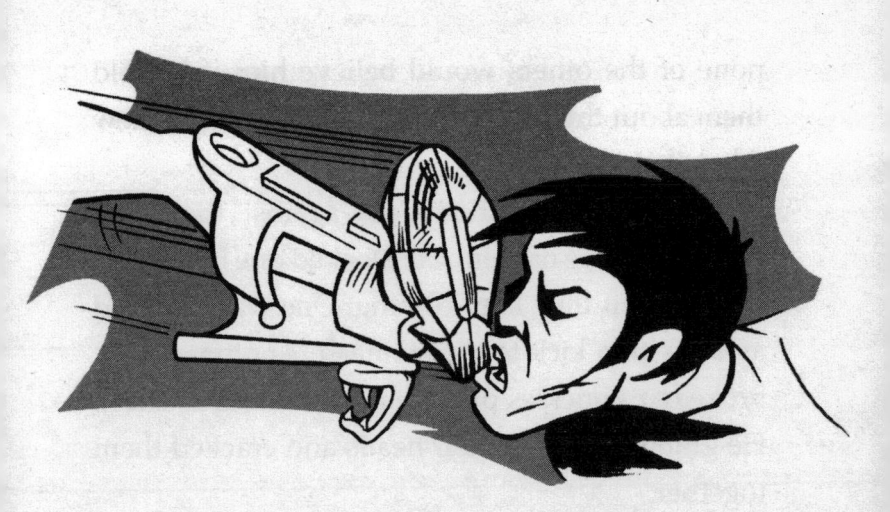

Rake spotted him just as the Vampire drew back his hand to hurl the knife at Snow.

'Look out!' he shouted at her.

Snow looked round, but her hands were trapped under the shield: she couldn't get free in time. The knife flew straight for her neck. She clenched her eyes shut. The dagger suddenly wobbled, swerved upwards and embedded itself in the ceiling. Rake stared, but then rushed to take out the knife-thrower as she fought back against the other one.

He would never forget what he had just seen. They all knew there was something . . . strange about Snow. Something slightly unnatural. But none of the others would believe him if he told them about this. He wondered if Snow even knew what she'd just done.

Oddball was pushed back against the ticket barriers by five of them. He blocked one blow after another, but they kept coming. One was knocked away with a kick to the stomach. Another nearly broke her knuckles punching his armoured chest. He grabbed two by their heads and cracked them together.

But one of the others managed to grab his hammer and started to hit him with it. His armour saved him from the worst of it. Oddball snatched the head of the hammer with one hand and seized the guy's wrist with the other. With one mighty heave, he hurled the man through the ticket barrier. Oddball kept hold of his hammer, but his opponent went crashing through the automatic gates, tumbling over into a heap on the other side.

The air filled with the sound of alarms. The ticket barrier lit up with flashing symbols.

'NO FARE PAID!' an electronic voice announced. 'NO FARE PAID! YOU ARE NOT AUTHORIZED TO ENTER THE STATION. INSERT VALID

TICKET! THE WHITE KNIGHTS HAVE BEEN SUMMONED. INSERT VALID TICKET NOW OR FACE ARREST AND/OR ON-THE-SPOT FINE!'

The fighting stopped. Everyone froze, staring at the offended ticket barrier.

'The White Knights are coming!' one of the Vampires cried.

Some of the other gang-members took up the cry. Their savage expressions were replaced by ones of fear. This small-time street gang did not want to mess with the White Knights.

'This isn't over!' their leader hissed at Rake.

Then they pulled away from the knights and ran like rabbits, spreading out and disappearing down the tunnels. The woman they had chased into the station was standing holding her left arm, which appeared to be wounded.

'You'd better come with us,' Rake said to her. 'The Kettles are almost as nasty to the *victims* of crime as they are to the *criminals*. If you don't want to end up being questioned in a cell aboard a Flying Fortress, follow us.'

She hesitated. But then she looked up at the flashing lights that were spreading down the ticket hall, and nodded. The knights started for the stairs that had brought them into the station earlier that evening, but she stopped them.

'Wait!' she called. 'That leads out into the car park! We'll be stuck out in the open. There's another way out down this tunnel!'

They turned to follow her down the subway, sprinting away from the alarm sirens and lights. Snow was last to follow her. The youngest and smallest of the knights paused, puzzled by what she was feeling.

Every instinct she had told her that they could not trust this woman.

Chapter 9
Talking to Strangers

They came to a halt in another part of the subway, listening carefully for the sound of anyone following them. But there was nothing.

'There's a set of stairs that comes out in a back street, out of sight of the shopping mall,' the woman told them, as she clutched her wounded arm.

'Thanks,' Rake said to her. 'Listen, what's your name? Where did you come from?'

'My name's Andrea,' she replied. 'I . . . I was out after curfew because my mother's power went out in her apartment and I went over to help. I'm an electrician, you see. There was some kind of weird explosion in the park she lives beside, and everyone's power went down. I got her fixed up, and I was on my way back when I took a wrong turn and ran into those lunatics. I think you saved my life back there.'

'Just doing our job, ma'am,' Hoax assured her. 'All in a night's work for the Cat People.'

Rake gave Hoax a hard look, but didn't say anything. Andrea tore a strip off her tunic and bound the wound on her left arm.

'You're hurt,' Snow said to Andrea, holding her hand out. 'I have a first-aid kit – I'm pretty good with injuries. Let me have a look at that for you.'

'No, it's OK,' Andrea replied, smiling. 'It's just a scratch. One of them tried to get his teeth into me, but I was able to fight him off.'

Snow nodded, but kept looking at the woman with suspicion. Andrea avoided her gaze by turning to face Rake.

'Thanks again,' she said. 'But who are you? You're not a gang like those Vampires, I can tell that much. What are you doing out after dark? You're running a terrible risk of being arrested by the White Knights.'

'No, we're not a gang,' Rake chuckled from behind his mask. 'We're—'

'We're just a group of cat-lovers, out looking for stray cats and giving them to good homes,' Hoax said, cutting in.

'But you're wearing armour under those cloaks,' Andrea said. 'I saw it when you were fighting.'

'That's because we're—' Rake began, but again, Hoax cut him off.

'That's because we're always running into gangs like the Vampires,' he informed her. 'It's a rough world out there. You've got to have protection, if you're going to wander around at night . . . saving those poor little cats.'

Rake was really staring at Hoax now. Snow moved up beside him, while Andrea was listening to Hoax. The youngest knight nudged her friend in the back. Rake looked at her and she shook her head.

'That's right,' Rake said, after glancing again at Snow. 'Cat conservation isn't taken seriously enough in this city. We're on a crusade to save the cats from the mean streets of Nu-Topia.'

'Right,' Andrea grunted. 'That's very noble of you. So where are you going now?'

'We have to head north,' Rake said. 'We have . . . we have to . . . The White Knights will be all over this area now. We have to get clear of them, if we're going to continue our work in peace.'

'I know the fastest way out of the area,' Andrea declared to all of them. 'But it's a bit risky. Actually, it's *very* risky. Personally, I wouldn't use it unless I was *desperate*.'

'The Cat People live for danger,' Hoax told her.

'Why don't you tell us about it?' Rake sighed.

The other knights stayed quiet, their faces hidden by their cat masks. If there was another way across the city, it was worth trying. Andrea looked around at them before continuing.

'Well, you know that the White Knights use Flying Fortresses to get around, right?' She waited for them all to nod. 'Right. Everybody knows that. But not everybody knows that they also have a private underground railway too. For when they need to get large numbers of troops across the city quickly, without anyone seeing them. Not many people know about it. I only know because I did some of the electrical wiring work in the tunnels.'

Andrea cast her eyes around them again, studying them.

'If you're serious about getting out of here as

fast as you can, that's the best way. The trains run back and forth all the time – there are hardly any cameras in the tunnels, and a lot of the time the trains are almost completely empty. From here, you can travel straight to Corporation Headquarters, or Nu-Topia Hospital, or the Academy, or even the outskirts of the city . . . and you'd be there in minutes.'

For a few moments, the knights didn't react. They looked at each other, then they all looked at Rake. He nodded, and turned to Andrea.

'How do we get in there?' he asked.

'There's an access tunnel not far from here. I can lead you there,' she replied. 'The only problem is, the trains are for transporting *White Knights*. So we have to get very close to one of their bases. We have to go right underneath the walls of a Peace Keep.'

'Of course we do,' Snow said quietly. Something about this woman and her story wasn't right, but Snow couldn't say what, so she didn't say anything more.

The subway brought them to the set of steps. From there, Andrea led them through some alleyways towards the Peace Keep. Tea-Leaf was looking around fearfully at the buildings that towered over them. As a thief, living in this city, she had never wandered this close to one of the police bases. But Andrea seemed to know where she was going. Only Snow was lagging behind, her hand brushing again and again over the handle of her baton.

Hoax stayed close to Andrea, asking her questions about her life. He was very curious about life outside the Academy, and she was one of the first Nu-Topians he had ever held a real conversation with. After a while, she started to get a bit irritated by it, but he kept at it. Rake was getting worried that Andrea might get suspicious. She might realize that the four Academy recruits knew very little about life in the city. She might even figure out where they were from.

'So, what kind of electrical work do you do?' Hoax asked her. 'Apart from White Knight train systems, I mean.'

'All sorts of things,' she answered. 'I do . . . erm, the wiring for holo-displays in shops – like the ones in the shopping mall.'

'The ones with all the ads?' Hoax exclaimed. 'That's cool. I wish I could do stuff like that. I'm just learning about electronics. You can pull all sorts of tricks with them.'

'I suppose you can,' Andrea sighed wearily. 'I've never thought of it that way.'

'Psst!' Tea-Leaf hissed. 'Fortress! Take cover!'

They were making their way along a narrow street lined with strange-shaped sculptures. All six of them ducked into the shadows of the sculptures nearest them. The huge white shape of the Flying Fortress soared past overhead.

It looked like an upturned battleship, nearly fifty metres long, with its biggest guns pointing towards the ground. The fearsome machine was mostly white, with black and silver detailing. It had short, stubby wings and its six engines were pointed almost straight down as it flew slowly, searching for anything suspicious.

Looking up at it from between the buildings on the street, they watched it glide past and out of sight.

'Close one,' Oddball muttered. 'I don't think they were really looking for us, or they'd have stopped to check out the street.'

'How far is it to the entrance to this place?' Rake asked.

'Not far now,' Andrea replied. 'We're almost there.'

She reached up to her ear as if to scratch it, but instead, she moved a pea-sized earphone to a more comfortable position in her ear. The hunting squad had already been alerted to the fact that she had found the Armouron Knights. Now, all she had to do was move everyone into position at the right time – and launch her attack. Hopefully, they might even take the young knights alive.

'Squad, this is Ulcer,' she whispered. 'They've taken the bait. Ten minutes away from ambush point. Let us through, then follow us in and wait for my signal. It'll be like shooting fish in a barrel.'

Ulcer looked back at the knights who were following her with such trust. She smiled at them.

'We're almost there,' she said again.

Chapter 10
Scouting the Way

The Peace Keep was a massive, hulking building with tall columns at the front and high walls all around it. It looked a bit like a Roman temple, but with a fortified wall lined with heavy guns and robot sentries. Two Flying Fortresses hovered overhead and a third one could be seen in the distance, just below the clouds.

'This could be a really, really dumb move,' Tea-Leaf muttered. She was crouching under the wing of a shuttle parked on an open piece of ground not far from the Keep. 'This secret train line better be easy to get into, Andrea. If we are spotted now, we won't have a hope of getting out of here.'

'Don't worry,' Andrea reassured her. 'Where

we're going, the White Knights won't even think to look for you. You don't need to worry about those toasters.'

The five knights stared at her in surprise.

'You know they're robots?' Rake exclaimed. 'I thought everyone living in Nu-Topia believed they were humans in armour.'

'What? Oh, yes . . . of course,' Andrea replied. 'They do. But I've worked on their train system, remember? I know more about them. That's how I know they won't come looking for us here. It wouldn't occur to them that someone might try to escape from them by coming this close to their base. They don't have the imagination for an idea like that. There's an underground car park under the building just down this street to our left. We can get into the tunnel system from there. There are no people in there at this time of night. There isn't even a security guard.'

'Yeah well, even so, I'm going to have a scout around,' Tea-Leaf said.

'No! No, wait!' Rake called after her.

'Back in a few minutes,' she told them, ignoring him.

The young thief ran quickly to the side of the

nearest building, tossing off her cloak and mask and pulling on her helmet. Leaving her disguise tucked under a car, she waited for her suit to match its colour to the building's shadows and then she darted away into the darkness.

'We shouldn't let her run off on her own like that,' Andrea commented. 'We could lose her.'

'She never does what she's told,' Rake said.

'Probably 'cos it's you that's doing the telling,' Oddball murmured.

'I heard that!' Rake snapped.

Tea-Leaf felt better now that she was on her own. She loved being with her team, but out here in the quiet darkness, she worked better alone. The entrance to the underground car park was blocked by a metal shutter. Tea-Leaf found a pedestrian entrance and picked the lock, silently opening the door. There were only a few lights on inside, just enough to see by. She waited inside the door for a minute, studying the ground floor through her visor, looking for anything that didn't fit.

Slowly, she moved further into the gloomy space, with its cold concrete walls. Two ramps on either side of the space led down to the next level. At the other side of ground floor, she could just see a doorway marked 'Staff Only'. Was that the way through, or did she need to head down one of the ramps? She lifted her visor and took a deep breath. Sometimes, she found her instincts worked better with the air on her face. Even down here, the way the air moved could tell her things.

Tea-Leaf was about to walk towards the nearest ramp when she heard something. Darting into the

shadow of a pillar, she peered out and gasped. Striding up the ramp were five figures, each dressed in the armour of an Armouron Knight. But she didn't recognize any of the suits. None of them could be from her team. She couldn't believe her eyes – there were other Armouron Knights on Earth.

But then she closed her visor down . . . and saw the truth.

Chapter 11
Ambushed

On board the *Invader*, Gland was in contact with the Byelons who were waiting to ambush the Armouron Knights. A light was pulsing on one of the side displays and the Byelon second-in-command tried to ignore it. That was the Chairman trying to get through. She had blocked the signal. But she knew that he knew that she was blocking the signal and that was just making him madder. She was hoping Ulcer would get back in time to deal with him.

Gland had no wish to take over as leader of the squad. The job was too stressful. The Chairman was the type who took offence easily. And people who offended him tended not to live very long. So

Gland found talking to the man to be a frightening experience, despite the fact that Byelons did not scare easily. Let Ulcer handle the life-threatening conversations, she thought. Organizing ambushes was much more to Gland's taste.

The knights were crossing the city at surprising speed, considering they were kids with hardly any experience. The squad had been tracking them, but Ulcer had found them in the end by sheer luck – she hadn't recognized them at first, in their Cat People costumes. And she hadn't counted on clashing with the Vampire gang, but the cunning shape-shifter had turned it to her advantage. Now she had the trust of the knights and it was going to cost them dear.

The Byelon leader had been sending short, regular reports whispered into her communicator, but things had been quiet for the last while.

'What's your status, Druel?' Gland asked over the communicator.

'We're still waiting,' Druel replied from his position at the ambush point. 'You sure these disguises will work?'

'They're alone and running scared in a dark city,' Gland said, smiling. 'They'll be desperate to find some friends. The disguises will work.'

She checked the clock and yawned. It was up to Ulcer now. All they could do was wait. It had been a long night and they had been on the go for several days – Gland was exhausted. Rubbing her eyes, she checked her screens again.

'According to Ulcer's tracking beacon, she's right outside,' Gland told Druel. 'It won't be long now. She'll give you the signal herself. Remember, try and take them alive.'

'That could be tough, if they put up a good fight,' he replied.

'Just do your best,' Gland told him. 'We can still get a good price for their dead bodies.'

'She's taking a really long time, isn't she?' Oddball said.

There was still no sign of Tea-Leaf. Oddball normally spoke quickly – perhaps because of all the different things going on in his overactive brain. But now he was getting nervous and was talking even faster than normal.

'We'd better go in and make sure she's OK,' Andrea said.

'The whole point of having a scout is that they

find the danger before the whole team walks into it,' Rake said. 'She can look after herself. We'll wait a few more minutes.'

'It's a trap!' Snow blurted out, suddenly grabbing hold of Andrea's arm and getting her in an armlock, so the woman couldn't move. 'It's her! She's not who she says she is. She's setting us up!'

'She's right,' Hoax growled. 'I know a liar when I hear one and she's been laying it on with a shovel. I think her story about the train system is true, but Tea-Leaf's probably walked right into trouble trying to find it.'

'I don't know what they're talking about!' Andrea protested to Rake, struggling against Snow's armlock. 'I'm just trying to help you because you saved my life. Why don't you believe me?'

Rake stared at her for a moment, then looked back at Snow and Hoax.

'No names from now on! You two stay here. Tie her hands and watch her.' He looked across at Oddball. 'We'll go inside. If we're not back out for you in five minutes . . . well, you'll probably need to come in and rescue us.'

Hoax took hold of Andrea while Snow took out her baton, which doubled as a gun for a grappling hook. She disconnected the top, pulled out some of the strong thin cord and cut a piece off. As she started tying Andrea's hands, Rake waved to Oddball and they crept out from under the wing of the shuttle. Then they crossed the street, found the door that Tea-Leaf had opened. They pushed the door open. It was dark inside.

There were a few lights on, but not enough to wash away all the shadows cast by the pillars, or the gloom gathered in the corners.

'Let's get rid of these masks and get our helmets on,' Rake whispered.

Just at that moment, he saw three figures on the far side of the garage. He moved forward trying to get a better look.

'They're wearing armour!' Oddball gasped. 'And they're not Gladiators – they're knights! Look at their medallions – their totems! They're Armouron Knights!'

The two boys walked out into the garage, still wearing their masks and cloaks. The three knights looked round, giving a start as if unsure what to make of the two cloaked figures.

'It's all right!' Rake called to them. 'We're Armouron! We're knights like you!'

'Stop!' a voice cried out from the shadows off to the left. It was Tea-Leaf. 'It's a trap! Put your helmets on!'

Rake and Oddball were already running for cover. From either side of the garage, laser beams cut through the air. As the shots forced Rake and Oddball into the cover of a low wall, the three knights came charging at them. Lasers exploded into the other side of the wall. They dumped their masks and cloaks. They got their helmets on and pulled their shields from their backs.

With their visors down, the two boys saw the three knights in their true forms. Byelon shape-shifters. Their slick bald, almost fish-like, heads and sagging chins, and their turquoise skin, were unmistakable. The three aliens were a frightening sight. There had to be at least two more shooting at them from either side. The boys only knew about Byelons by reputation. But Salt had told them that the Chairman had shape-shifters working for him as spies and assassins.

'Ah, japes!' Rake swore. 'All right – Stand Together!'

'Battle as One!' Oddball growled back.

They felt the power of their totems flowing through their armour, through their bodies. The three Byelons were almost on top of them, armed with stun-batons and carrying laser blasters in holsters on their hips. The lasers stopped firing from the sides of the garage as the three assassins reached the wall the two boys were hiding behind.

With the power of his Armouron totem sending energy surging through his tired limbs, Rake came up behind his shield and whipped his sword handle out so that it extended into a lance. He whacked it down on the shoulder of the first attacker, knocking the baton from her hand. Oddball dived over the wall right into the path of the second assassin, rolled and swung his hammer up into the Byelon's chest. The shape-shifter had the air driven from his lungs and fell backwards.

The third one got a blow in on Oddball's helmet, knocking him over, and then swung his baton back at Rake, who blocked it with his shield. The knight rammed the butt of his lance into the Byelon's ribs and drove a kick into the shape-shifter's chest just as Oddball keeled over behind him. The Byelon

toppled over onto the floor and Oddball, still dazed from the blow, punched the assassin in the head with his gauntlet-covered fist.

The first one to attack was still on her feet, however. She jumped at them, delivering a flying kick to Rake's chest, sending him backwards over the wall. He lost his grip on his lance and shield. She kicked Oddball in the stomach and then grabbed his armoured head and smacked it against the wall.

Leaping over the wall, she had her legs swept

out from under her by Rake's arm. He went to get her in a ground-hold, but she drew her blaster. Even as she pointed it straight at his visor, Oddball's shield came down on her head, knocking her out. She slumped on top of Rake, who pushed her over onto the ground.

Oddball barely got his shield up in time as more laser blasts were fired at them. The shots thudded into the shield hard enough for him to feel the impacts up to his shoulder. The last two Byelons were running across the garage at them. Three more shots burned through the air, one striking Oddball in the thigh, scarring his armour. The others hit Rake on his shield and across his shoulder. Again, only his armour saved him from injury.

A crossbow bolt whacked the gun out of the hand of one of the shape-shifters. Then Tea-Leaf swung down from a beam in the ceiling, grabbed the other one around the neck with her feet and flipped him onto his back. The shape-shifter's partner pulled his baton out to hit Tea-Leaf. But Rake hurled his shield, catching the Byelon in the stomach and knocking him flying.

Some of the others were already starting to

recover. Tea-Leaf picked up Rake's shield and sprinted across to her friends.

'That was too close,' she said, handing over the shield. 'Sorry, I couldn't get back out. They had the door covered.'

As the three real knights made their way towards the door, they discovered the Byelons weren't finished yet. The heavy steel door was locked – and its lock had been fused by a laser blast. They couldn't open it. Behind them, the Byelons were getting to their feet.

'Ah, dunk!' Rake growled. 'They're good, I'll give 'em that.'

Raising their shields and weapons, they turned to face the five shape-shifters. And the Byelons raised their blasters. The three knights wondered how many shots it would take to puncture their shields and their armour – how many it would take to kill them.

Chapter 12
Running Battle

Rake, Oddball and Tea-Leaf stared down the five barrels of their enemies' guns. They weren't going to give up without a fight. But then the fight was taken out of their hands. There was a loud bang from behind them, making them jump. Something hit the door once, then again and again. It bent and buckled and then the lock gave way.

The three knights had just enough time to jump aside before a horde of Cat People came crashing through, smashing the battered door out of their way. The five shape-shifters were still in their disguises – as Armouron Knights. They were taken completely by surprise as nearly thirty maniacs in cloaks and cat masks rushed towards them. Closely followed by a gang of yowling cats. The Cat People were all armed with sticks and clubs.

'That's them!' their leader, Ginger, snarled as he pointed at the shape-shifter 'knights'. He turned to his gang: 'Their armour won't save them this time! Attack!'

Rake, Oddball and Tea-Leaf watched in a daze as the Byelons turned and ran with the Cat People chasing after them.

'This would be a great time to get out of here,' Tea-Leaf pointed out.

'Absolutely,' Rake said, nodding. 'Let's go.'

They were almost through the door when one of the Cat People happened to look back.

'Wait!' she shrieked, loud enough to make her gang turn round. 'There's two of them right there! And that one there kicked me into a potted plant!'

The Cat People let out more yowls and most of them turned round to come after the young knights. They looked like easier targets – these three didn't have guns.

Tea-Leaf was already sprinting across the road, with Rake and Oddball on her heels. Hoax and

Snow had thrown off their Cat People disguises and had their helmets on. They dragged Andrea to her feet as the other three reached them. Seen through their visors, it was obvious to all of them that she too was a Byelon.

'Who are you?' Rake shouted at her, grabbing her by her collar and shaking her.

'Who am I?' she sneered, lifting her chin to look down her nose at him. 'My name is Ulcer, *boy*. And I'm your worst nightmare. Let me go now, while you still have the chance.'

'Everybody's making threats tonight,' he said, pushing her away.

The Cat People were racing across the road. The knights were tired. There was no way they could keep running for much longer. Rake gritted his teeth and strode out to meet the gang, but Snow grabbed his arm.

'We can't fight them,' she said to him. 'There's too many of them and we're too close to the Keep.'

Rake looked up at the Peace Keep, filled with White Knights, just a street away. Snow was right. So they all started running again, dragging their captive with them. But the Cat People were fast.

They snatched and struck out at the knights as they ran. Tea-Leaf led the way, Snow and Oddball pulled Ulcer along, Rake and Hoax stayed at the back, keeping the attackers at bay.

But they were fighting a losing battle. The hunt would not last long.

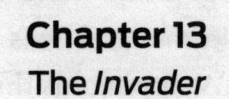

Chapter 13
The *Invader*

Back in the park where all the trouble had started, peace had settled over the whole area. The fires in the trees had been put out. The White Knights had restored order. The war machine known as the *Invader* was invisible and silent, hidden from the people of Nu-Topia.

An old homeless man crawled out of the box that served as his house. He was nearly seventy years old. He had lived rough in that park for nearly two of those years. His box was deep in the trees, where it could not be seen. Even the White Knights, who always rounded up the homeless and took them away, didn't think to look in this part of the wood.

The old man was a very deep sleeper. He had not been woken by the explosions, or the screams, or the announcements by the White Knights. If he had, he would still have stayed where he was. This was the closest thing he had to a home and he did not want to be taken away.

He always came out early in the morning to play with his dog, while there was still no one around. The little mongrel was old, but not as old as its owner. Wrapping his three coats around him, the ragged man shivered against the cold and walked out of the trees. He threw the ball for the dog and the dog brought it back to him. After the third or fourth throw, he was quite far out into the middle of the park.

The next time he threw the ball, it seemed to hit an invisible wall. The old man blinked. Were his eyes lying to him? He shuffled closer and reached out his hand. It was true. There was an invisible wall here. There were even dents in the ground where the huge thing had landed. He rapped on it with his knuckles.

Something came alive, high above him. There came the sound of machinery whirring, clanking. A humming started, growing into a loud whine.

Gun turrets swivelled to centre the old homeless man in their sights.

The war machine was about to open fire when a signal came through on the communicator in the *Invader*'s control room. Gland had fallen asleep. She heard the beeping signal, let out a gasp and woke up. Then she noticed the displays flashing and saw that the machine had armed its guns. She reached over, switched the controls to manual, and turned off the guns. She wondered which of the Chairman's engineers had designed this machine. Whoever it was should have their head examined. It was way too jumpy. Anything seemed to set it off.

The communicator was still beeping. She answered it.

'Yes, Ulcer?'

Ulcer's voice was almost drowned out by what sounded a lot like a street battle.

'What took you so long to answer?' her leader hissed. 'The ambush failed. They've captured me. Come and get me, Gland. Track my signal. Find me. And Gland? Destroy anything or anyone who gets in your way, do you hear me?'

'I hear you,' Gland told her, reaching across to

start the engines. 'I've got your signal locked in. I'll be there in less than ten minutes.'

The old man was staggering back to try and get a better look at what he couldn't see when he heard four massive engines starting up. He began hobbling back towards the trees, but he was too slow. A blast of jet thrusters picked him up and tossed him several metres into the trees. Something lifted off behind him, but when he turned to look, he still couldn't see anything. As the wind blew back his long grey hair, he wailed and crawled for cover. His dog howled at the sky. But the invisible thing was gone.

Chapter 14
'We Meet Again'

Oddball heard the last part of Ulcer's message. He slowed down just enough to grab her by the back of the neck and pull the earphone from her ear.

'Dunk!' he shouted. 'Hey, we've got more trouble coming! Ulcer here has called in reinforcements!'

Rake smacked away a stick that was being swung at his head. He tripped up one of the cat gang with his lance. Then he glanced desperately at Oddball.

'Reinforcements from *where*?' he panted. 'You mean the Kettles?'

Oddball shrugged, but Snow was staring at Ulcer, a strange look in her eyes.

'No, it's that *war machine*, isn't it?' she snapped. 'That's why you're out here after us. You were on board that thing, weren't you? You were *in charge* of it. And now it's coming for you.'

Ulcer didn't have time to answer. Tea-Leaf had just led them round a corner in the alley they were running through. They found the way blocked. Standing in their path was a group of nearly twenty young men and women. Each one was dressed in a black suit, white shirt and waistcoat, red cravat and a black cloak with a red lining. Fake fangs protruded from each red-lipped mouth.

The knights came to an abrupt halt, as did the Cat People who came round the corner after them.

'So, Cat People, we meet again,' the leader of the Vampires said.

'We do?' the leader of the Cat People replied in a puzzled voice.

'You caught us by surprise last time,' the Vampire leader told them. 'This time, we're ready for you.'

All the Vampires carried sticks, clubs or swords. They started to move towards their new enemies. Rake looked over at Snow, who pointed her thumb back at the Cat People. That was who the Vampires were after. Rake nodded. He gently moved Ulcer, Oddball and Tea-Leaf over to the side of the alley. Snow took Hoax's arm and led him to the other side. The two gangs ignored them.

With a chorus of shouts, shrieks, yowls and snarls, the Vampires and the Cat People jumped on each other. Rake hauled Ulcer with him as he slid along the wall, trying to avoid the fight. The five knights and their captive came out the other end of the alley and started walking quickly away from the battle-scene.

There came the sound of sirens and running feet. The noise had attracted the attention of the White Knights. That fight wasn't going to last very long.

Ulcer swore to herself as they hurried away from the street battle. The Chairman would be having a fit by now. There was no way Gland would be able to talk her way out of this mess – their boss would be demanding to know what was going on. And if he discovered Ulcer had lied about the knights so she could go after them herself, he'd have her head for it.

The march of hundreds of armoured boots

tramping through the streets made a sound like no other. The White Knights were spreading out through the area, their cold eyes searching, their weapons ready.

Staying out of sight as much as they could, the young knights took one turn after another, trying to avoid the android police and the street cameras. There was less than two hours until sunrise. They were almost ready to give up hope that they would ever get home.

They were crossing a dark street when a laser blast blew out a shop window behind them. They all dropped to the ground and started crawling for any cover they could find. Another shot punched a hole in the road, leaving a large crater. Rake and Hoax were scrambling towards a parked van when a rain of rapid-fire shots drilled a line of holes in the road and then blew up the van. It was thrown into the air, flames bursting out of it, before it crashed down again, only metres from them, nearly crushing them.

'ARMOURON KNIGHTS,' a voice called from high above them. 'RELEASE YOUR PRISONER AND SURRENDER. I WILL ONLY TELL YOU ONCE.'

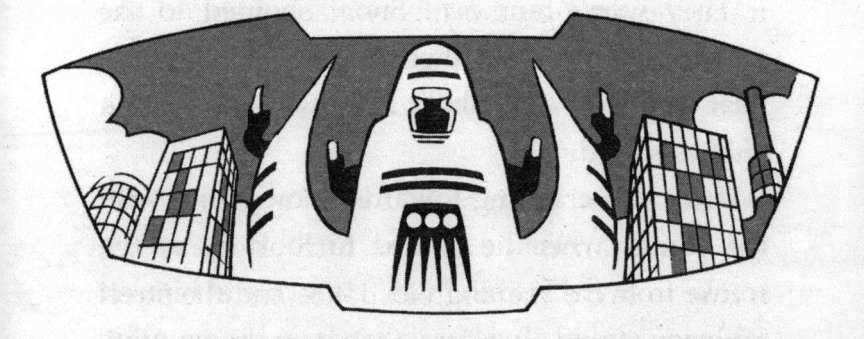

There, in the night sky above them, was the war machine. Its jet engines were nearly completely silent, and they could only see it because of their Armouron visors. To the rest of the world, it was invisible.

The five knights looked helplessly at one another. There didn't seem to be any way out of this. This thing had enough firepower to kill them all, no matter where they hid.

'That thing has jet engines,' Oddball said to Rake. 'I know how to make jet engines explode.'

'You probably know how to make *water* explode,' Rake called back. 'Any idea how to get past all the big huge guns?'

'Er . . . no,' Oddball admitted.

It was Snow who acted first. She wrapped her arm around Ulcer's neck and pulled her in close.

'They won't hurt *her*,' Snow shouted to the others. 'I think she's their leader. Get in close. That way, they can't shoot at us without the risk of hitting her.'

Hoax was crawling towards Snow along with the others, when he turned to look up at the smoke from the burning van. He swore at himself for being stupid. Twisting a catch on his gauntlet, he fired two smoke bombs from the tiny, spring-loaded launchers in the arm of his armour. They burst against the ground, spewing smoke out over the street. Now the machine would have trouble seeing who was who.

The *Invader* hovered down lower, its jet thrusters starting to blow away the smoke. Its guns moved around, searching for a target. But by the time the smoke had cleared, the five knights and their captive were gone. The cover of a manhole lay slightly crooked across the round hole. The Armouron Knights had taken to the sewers.

Chapter 15
Into the Stink

'Some day,' Tea-Leaf said, as she led the group down the stinking tunnel, 'the Kettles are going to start putting cameras and patrols down here too.'

'I don't want to sound like a complete wuss here.' Hoax coughed, 'but I think this smell is seeping straight into my brain.'

'Close the filters on your helmet, you rump,' Oddball told him.

Hoax did as he was told, and most of the smell was filtered out. The tunnel they were walking through was just high enough for them to stand in, its curved walls highest in the middle. They were striding along a metal walkway, which hung over the river of sewage flowing along the bottom of the tunnel. The stench was incredible. The walls were coated in some kind of grey-green slime. The only light came from the grates in the ceiling that opened out into the street above.

'Our suits are going to smell of this for ages after we get out of here,' Snow groaned. 'Do you remember how much swearing the master did last time we had to drag our backsides through the sewers?' She was careful not to mention Salt's name in front of Ulcer. 'He said we'd be scrubbing our own armour from now on.'

'You hear that?' Hoax grumbled at Ulcer. 'I'm going to be cleaning sewage out of the grips in my boots with a toothbrush because of you. So just try and escape, dough-face. Just give me an excuse to flatten you.'

The kids sometimes wondered if Salt cared more about their armour than he did about them – or at least that was how it seemed sometimes, when he was in a bad mood. It didn't help when Hoax asked daft questions, like why armour mounted with super-powered totems still had to be cleaned with a brush.

Ulcer said nothing. She had shed her disguise,

but her hands were still tied behind her back, so she couldn't cover her face. She was trying not to breathe through her nose.

'Do you know where we're going?' Rake asked Tea-Leaf.

'It's only a guess,' she replied. 'I don't know this part of the sewer system. It's really easy to get lost down here. But I think this tunnel is taking us back towards the shopping mall.'

'We're never going to get home,' Oddball grumbled. 'And that thing is probably still up there somewhere.'

'It is,' Snow said, looking up at the ceiling of the tunnel. She held her gloved hand up, as if feeling for something. 'It hasn't gone away. Can't you sense the way it's searching for us?'

None of the knights replied. They were becoming used to Snow and her funny ways. Oddball looked down at the tiny earphone in his hand – the one he had taken from Ulcer.

'We should get rid of this,' he said to Rake. 'That machine could be tracking it. And if they're able to use phones and machines in the city, that means Ulcer's working with the White Knights. They could be picking it up too.'

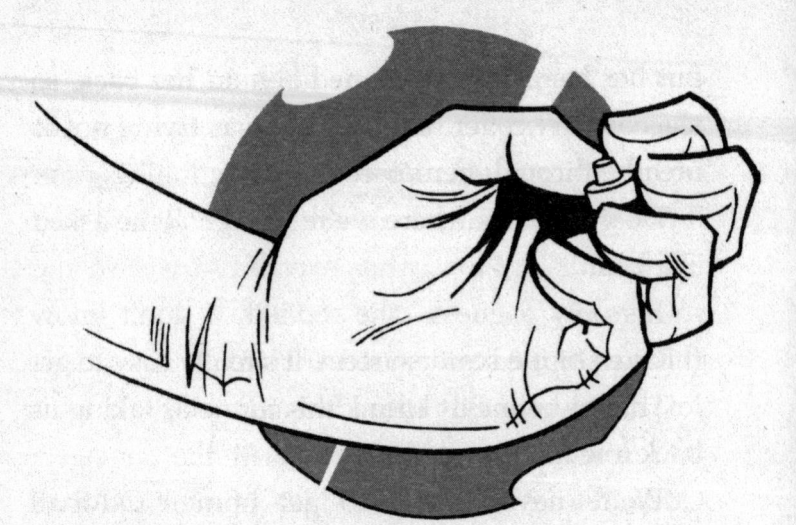

Rake took it from him and studied it.

'I'm tired of just trying to escape all the time,' he muttered, almost to himself. 'I'm sick of running.'

'Running is the only thing you *can* do,' Ulcer snorted. 'And you won't be doing that for long. My squad will find us. They're searching for me even now. You won't even see our gunship, the *Invader*, coming until it's too late. Give yourselves up now, and you might still be alive when we hand you over to the Chairman.'

' "Running is the only thing you *can* do,"' Hoax said, imitating her voice. 'Yeah, right. If we die, *you'll* die with us, dough-face. That machine . . .

that *Invader*, hasn't blown holes in the road to reach us down here because we have *you*.' He put on her voice again, pointing at the stinking gunk flowing by beneath them: 'Shut up now and you might still be alive when we throw you in the sewage.'

Rake stopped and stared at Hoax.

'That gives me an idea,' he said.

'You're going to throw her in the sewage?' Oddball asked. 'How is that going to help? Mind you, it would be fun watching her go in.'

'No.' Rake shook his head, looking at Oddball. 'Listen, you said you knew how to make jet engines explode, right? You weren't kidding, were you?'

'No way,' Oddball declared in his usual, hyperactive voice. 'A jet engine needs to suck in air to make it work. Those huge engines on the *Invader* have air intakes – turbofans – at one end and the jet thrust blasts out the other. Any big object that gets sucked in by the turbofans will jam up the engine and make it blow up. It's easy enough – but you have to get pretty close to do it.'

'I know how to get us close,' Rake replied. He

turned to Tea-Leaf. 'We have to get back to the shopping mall. There are a few things there we're going to need.'

Tea-Leaf nodded, stopped at the next junction, and made a quick decision. Pointing down the right tunnel, she waved them on. They picked up the pace, hurrying down the dark, smelly passageway. The footsteps echoed along the concrete walls.

'Clack of a time to go shopping,' Hoax commented, as they disappeared round a bend.

Chapter 16
Meeting at the Mall

The five young knights were faced with three tough choices. For a start, they should have been trying to get home as fast as they possibly could. But they couldn't risk travelling through the city now. After the big gang-fight and the attack by the *Invader*, the White Knights would be out in force. It would be next to impossible to find a route through the streets.

Their second choice was to go through the sewers. But it was a maze down there. Tea-Leaf didn't know this part of the system and they could get lost. They might end up wandering around for days.

They were getting nervous now. There was just

over an hour before sunrise. Back at the Academy, some of the instructors would be up soon. It wouldn't take long before someone noticed that Rake, Hoax, Snow and Oddball were missing. And once the sun came up, five knights in suits of armour would be easily spotted. They would have to hide somewhere for the whole day.

The Academy would be put on alert. Someone might even start asking questions. They could make a connection between the five knights that had been seen in the city that night, and the four Gladiator cadets who were missing.

So Rake had come up with a third choice. He wanted to damage the *Invader* badly enough to stop the Byelons from hunting them. And he wanted to make such a big loud mess when they did it, that the White Knights would come running from all over the area.

That would mean fewer patrols on the streets. Which might make it a bit easier for the five knights to get home.

'Ah, dunk,' Tea-Leaf grunted. 'It's worth a try.'

So when they reached a service tunnel that led into the shopping mall, Rake explained his plan. He had noticed something when they knocked out a few of the Byelons in the fight in the underground car park. The Byelons had not changed back to their normal shapes. They kept their disguises.

He told Ulcer to change – he wanted her to look like him. She refused . . . until he threatened her with his sword. Then spots appeared all over her skin, spreading and turning into lumps that covered her, settling down into her new shape. The Byelon looked like Rake's twin. He smiled at her – and then he hit her over the head with the butt of his sword, knocking her out.

Oddball, Hoax and Tea-Leaf carried the unconscious shape-shifter out onto the main concourse. They stretched her body out on the ground. Her hands and feet were still tied. Right above them, three floors up, was the food-court. Rake led Snow up there. He looked over the rail. He tilted his head and then waved at them to move Ulcer a little to the right. They dragged her over as he'd directed, and he gave them the thumbs-up sign.

Above him, through the massive glass and steel ceiling, they could see the sky was starting to grow lighter with the approach of dawn.

Then the other two boys raced back up the stairs to the food-court. Tea-Leaf stayed down there, under the shadow of a footbridge. It was her job to keep an eye on Ulcer, in case the Byelon woke up and realized what was going on. Rake and Snow were busy pulling chairs, tables and parasols towards the railing.

'All right, we're ready,' Rake declared, taking a deep breath. 'Let's make the call. If they're tracking Ulcer's phone, the *Invader* won't be far away.'

Hoax took his helmet off and Rake handed him the earphone. Hoax put it in his ear. He was about to speak, then he turned to Rake as if to ask him something.

'The one controlling the ship?' Oddball said. 'I think her name is Gland.'

Hoax made an 'ah' shape with his mouth and nodded. Then he activated the earphone.

'Gland?' he said, doing an impression of Ulcer's voice. 'Do you hear me?'

The signal went straight through to the *Invader*. Gland was quick to reply.

'Ulcer? Are you all right?'

'Better than all right,' Hoax replied. 'I've broken

free. I've captured one of them. I'm going after the others now – they're all in the shopping mall. You can come in and pick up the one in the red and black armour. He's all tied up for you. I've left him out on the main concourse.'

'Right away, Ulcer,' Gland called back. 'The squad is back on board. I'll send them in on foot.'

'No, no!' Hoax snapped, looking at Rake. 'The knights are trying to set up an ambush for the squad. Don't worry about being quiet. Bring the *Invader* straight in. Pick the prisoner right up from the concourse. Let's show these kids what real power looks like.'

'Yes, Ulcer. We're on our way.'

The phone went dead. Hoax bit his lip and looked around at the others.

'They're on their way,' he said.

Chapter 17
Taking the Bait

At the end of the main concourse was a huge wall of glass looking out over one of the car parks. The *Invader* appeared in the sky, soaring over the plain of empty parking spaces. It approached quickly, gun turrets swivelling in search of targets as it closed on the mall. It hardly slowed down as it crashed through the massive window in an explosion of glass.

Ulcer lay on the floor, less than a hundred metres away, still disguised as Rake. The *Invader* glided towards her. Tea-Leaf crouched behind a pillar nearby, her eyes fixed on the shape-changer. Above her, the other four knights watched the war machine slow down as it drew near. They waited for the moment to strike.

Tea-Leaf lifted her head as she saw Ulcer move. The wind from the jet engines was waking her up. As the *Invader* drifted overhead, Ulcer shook her head and looked around. She tried to move, but her hands and feet were bound. Tea-Leaf tightened her grip on her crossbow as she saw the alien begin to change shape.

The *Invader* came to a halt, hovering in the air above Ulcer. Its huge weight was held up by the force of its jet thrusters. They were pointing straight down, which meant the turbofans that fed them air at the other end were pointing straight up. And one of them was right below the balcony of the food court.

'Now!' Rake shouted.

Ulcer was a world-class assassin. Without someone holding onto her, she wasn't going to stay tied up for long. She changed back into her normal form – her arms and legs were thinner now. The cords were looser on her wrists and ankles. She began to twist them back and forth, working them free. The blast from the *Invader*'s engines nearly blew her across the floor, but she lay flat, finally freeing her wrists. In another couple of seconds, she had her ankles free. The Byelon leader raised herself up waved at the machine.

Even as she was doing this, Rake, Oddball, Snow and Hoax stood up, grabbing the edges of a table. With one great heave, they hurled it off the balcony and out towards the air intake of the nearest engine. The suction seemed to catch the table, drawing it in, but suddenly the machine moved, rising up, and the table tumbled to the ground below.

'Try again – fast!' Rake yelled.

He and Hoax picked up another table, Oddball and Snow seized chairs. They all threw the furniture towards the turbofan. But it was too late: the furniture smashed against the armoured sides of the engine. Ulcer was waving the machine away from the balcony, out of their reach.

'Dunk it, just give us one more chance!' Rake growled. 'Just one more chance!'

The machine swooped back down, a ramp dropping from its base to pick up Ulcer. Tea-Leaf came out from behind her pillar, attaching a strong cord to the bolt of her crossbow. She took aim at Ulcer, intending to nab her with the cord.

The machine could blow them all away . . . unless she could snatch back their prisoner and scare off Ulcer's team-mates.

Tea-Leaf didn't have a clear shot. With the blast from the jet engines, she had to get close or her bolt would just be blown off target. Ulcer made it to the ramp and jumped on. Tea-Leaf swore to herself and moved further out. The crew of the *Invader* spotted her. Their guns turned on Tea-Leaf. Explosions started to burst on the floor around her. The machine came in towards her.

'They're going to kill her!' Rake roared.

Snow watched the *Invader* swing round to close on Tea-Leaf. It stayed well clear of the balcony. The youngest knight judged the distance and snapped open her shield, making it three times its normal size. Standing up straight, she spun round twice and hurled the shield like a discus. It soared out over the concourse, heading towards one of the engines. But then the *Invader* moved again, shifting sideways, the pilot sensing the danger. The shield was going to miss.

Snow let out a frustrated scream. The shield suddenly swerved, changing direction, as if steered by an invisible hand. The others glanced

in amazement at Snow and then turned their eyes back to the gunship. The shield flew over the mouth of one of the turbofans and was sucked down abruptly into the spinning blades.

An explosion burst out from under the blades, sending many of them shooting through the air like spears. The knights took cover as more detonations rippled through the engine. The *Invader* shook and tilted to one side. Debris from the exploding engine punched holes into two of the other engines. They, in turn, began to bulge and shudder with spouts of fire bursting out of them.

The war machine leaned over further. Its remaining engine was no longer able to support its weight. It hit the ground, crushing the gun turrets on its base. It dug a trench across the paved floor of the concourse as it dragged its tail, struggling to lift off again.

'It's coming straight for us!' Hoax shouted.

They dived clear just as the *Invader*'s massive weight drove into the balcony, falling through and taking most of it with it. The gunship finally stopped short as it gouged a hole in three floors of designer stores.

Chapter 18
The Aftermath

The five young knights walked through the clouds of dust and smoke. They gazed at the wreckage of the monstrous machine. All around them, pieces of wall and ceiling were still crumbling to the floor. Shards of glass were falling from the roof high above them.

For a moment, it was very quiet. Then Rake let out a wild scream, making them all jump. He raised his fists and whooped again.

'Yeeesssss! Yes, yes, yeeeessss! We did it!'

Hoax thumped him on the shoulder.

'You trying to give me a clackin' heart attack?' he snapped.

Rake ignored him, and bounced around,

punching the air and shouting in triumph.

'Rake,' Snow said to him. She tried again: 'Rake? Hey . . . Rake!'

He stopped and looked at her.

'We should go,' she said, pointing at the nearest door.

'Oh. Yeah, right,' he replied sheepishly and turned to follow the others. 'OK, but that was still BRILLIANT! Did you see that? I mean – of course you did. But, WOW! *We* did that! And that *throw*, Snow. That was incredible!'

'That was *impossible*,' Oddball muttered.

'I was just lucky,' Snow said in a coy voice. 'It probably just caught in the wind from the engines or something.'

'No, it didn't,' Oddball said under his breath.

Tea-Leaf met them in the corridor. She was almost as fired up as Rake. She let out a shriek when she saw them and tried to hug all of them at once.

'That was BRILLIANT!' she shouted, even though they could all hear her perfectly well. '*We* did that! That was amazing! And Snow . . . wow, what a throw!'

'I think it just caught on the wind,' Snow sighed modestly.

Rake had started to calm down. They still had to get home. Salt would be growling about their poor timekeeping, but they were sure he'd be pleased enough with the havoc they had caused to the Chairman's plans for that fancy gunship. And their master would be hugely relieved to have them home . . . even if he didn't show it. But it was time to go. The White Knights would be rushing here from all over the area. The Armouron had to disappear fast.

It took them less than fifteen minutes to run through the sewers to the car park where Ulcer had launched her ambush. There, they found an entrance into the White Knights' underground railway system, just as she had described.

There were hardly any cameras, and most of the android police were up in the streets, dealing with the fallout from the *Invader*'s destruction. The five knights crept into a freight carriage going in the right direction.

Shivering and exhausted, they huddled in the dark, lost in their thoughts. Now that the action was over, the weariness and cold set in. They felt more like tired kids than armoured warriors.

Hoax and Snow stared at the wall, thinking

about the sleep they wouldn't get when they made it back to the Academy. The four cadets had a full day's Gladiator training ahead of them.

Tea-Leaf knew she could sleep, but she also wanted to get back out on the streets as soon as she could. She wanted to hear about how this disaster for the Perfect Corporation would change things in the city.

Oddball and Rake were both staring at Snow. Oddball's scientific mind had seen Snow's miraculous throw for what it was. He felt a mixture of amazement, jealousy and fear at the power that Snow seemed to have.

Rake had always suspected that Snow was more than she seemed. And he doubted this young girl, whom he had known for most of her short life, even suspected how extraordinary – and dangerous – she might be. Both boys gazed at her and wondered how this could affect the fates of the Armouron.

As the five stowaways rode the police train home to the Academy, they realized they were becoming more than just their master's students. They had faced a cunning, deadly enemy on their own – and they had won.

The train slowed. Outside, through the narrow windows, they saw the walls of the station marked with the Academy logo. From here, it would be an easy matter to sneak from these underground tunnels into the Old School, where Salt would be waiting. They were home.

Chapter 19
Counting the Cost

Ulcer and her squad of assassins dragged themselves from the wreckage of the *Invader*. The sloping floor of a shop balcony allowed them to slide to the floor of the concourse. There, they found themselves surrounded by White Knights. Looking up through the broken glass of the roof, they could see three Flying Fortresses hovering overhead.

A cordon had been set up around the shopping mall. It was sealed off from the public. Nobody would be shopping there for some time. A White Knight strode up to the battered Byelons. The robot wore the black markings of a captain – the highest officer rank in the android police.

But right now, it was just a messenger. A light appeared in a lens in its chest and a hologram of the Chairman blinked into life.

'I hired you to do a simple job,' he said, his voice low with barely controlled anger. 'I have to say, I am not at all happy with how you have handled your task. I have just discovered that the rebels you fought with were Armouron Knights – and you did not feel it necessary to inform me at the time.' He paused, and Ulcer thought she detected a hint of fear in his voice. 'World-class assassins armed with a high-tech gunship and they still defeated you. I demand an explanation. You will come here in person and provide it.'

The hologram of the Chairman pointed at the ruined war machine.

'And you owe me for the loss of the gunship,' he added. 'The damage to the shopping mall is also very great. It will take you a long time to make back the money you have cost me. I promise you that the work I give you to earn back that money . . . will be as unpleasant as possible.'

The hologram shimmered and disappeared. Ulcer scowled. The White Knight stood there, as if waiting for her to say something, but there was nothing to say. She hated robots, especially these android police. Waving to her squad, they walked away through the circle of White Knights. She despised the Chairman, but she needed his money. And she didn't want him as an enemy. She and her team would have to put up with whatever humiliation he dished out – for now.

The Byelon assassins had never been faced with such an embarrassing defeat. She would not stand for that. No matter what it took, she would make the Armouron Knights pay for what they had done. And Ulcer swore an oath to herself that it would be a terrible revenge.

If you enjoyed *Lying Eyes*,
you might like a sneak preview of the
next book in the series: *The Caged Griffin*.
Turn over for the first few pages . . .

THE CAGED GRIFFIN

Richard Dungworth

A BANTAM BOOK 978 0 553 82196 3
Copyright © RDF Media Ltd/Armouron Ltd, 2010

Chapter 1
Bruisers and Losers

'Get a move on, you idiot!'

Stamper gave the black-haired boy crouching at his feet an impatient cuff around the head.

'I need to be ready to fight *now*, not in a week's time!'

The boy's shoulders tensed beneath his tunic. He was struggling to keep his temper.

What wouldn't I give to smack him one in his ugly mug, thought Rake bitterly. He snapped shut the last magna-buckle on Stamper's left leg guard. *Half a season in the Arena and he thinks he's it . . .*

He reached for the matching greave lying beside him – the final part of Stamper's armour.

If you can call it that. Rake turned the leg guard over in his hands. Compared to his own unique body armour – which right now was safely stowed in its hiding place – Stamper's seemed crude and clumsy. This showy stuff was what all the Academy Gladiators wore. It might look flashy, but Rake would take his own ultra-light, ultra-tough suit any day.

'I said, *hurry up!*'

A jab from Stamper's toe-cap brought Rake's mind back to the job in hand. Trying to keep his cool, he fitted the greave against the Gladiator's hefty shin and began fastening its buckles. With the last one done, he stood up.

'About time!' Stamper snarled at him. 'Just my luck to be kitted out by a dunk-head like you and your klutz of a sidekick!'

A pale, flame-haired boy stood beside Rake. He was weighed down with the rest of Stamper's equipment. This included a helmet, a shield and a slingshock – a throwing weapon comprising two heavy balls linked by a length of chain.

The boy responded to Stamper's insult with a cheery grin.

But Rake felt his temper flare again. 'Great

put-down,' he said sarcastically under his breath. 'Calling me and Hoax names must make you feel real tough.'

Stamper lunged forward. His livid face was only centimetres from Rake's.

'Don't get smart with me, *cadet!*' he spat. 'You may *think* you're some sort of big-shot, but until you make Gladiator – if there's any chance a no-hoper like you ever *will* – you're just here to do my dirty work. Understood?'

A hush had fallen across the Attiring Chamber. Half a dozen other Gladiators were getting ready for the day's programme of beast-battling, competitions and one-on-one combat. They each had a pair of cadet attendants to assist them. All had stopped working to watch the promising face-off between Rake and Stamper.

But a moment later the tension was broken by a loud buzz that filled the chamber – the first time signal. On cue, a group of seven low podiums rose smoothly from the chamber floor. Each was brightly lit from underneath.

'You're on, big fella!' beamed Hoax, offering Stamper his equipment.

Stamper held Rake's fiery gaze for another long

🛡 ⚜ 🔱 ◉ 🏛 🅰 🔆 ◈ ◉ ✴

second, then pushed him away with a dismissive grunt.

'Later, loser!'

He snatched his helmet from Hoax and put it on. Grasping the slingshock's chain in one heavy fist and his shield in the other, he strode towards the glowing platforms.

Stamper and his fellow Gladiators each mounted a podium. The buzzer sounded for a second time. Seven circular apertures opened in the chamber's

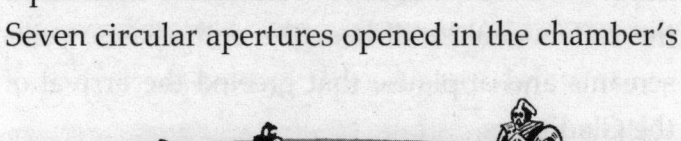

high ceiling. Through the openings, the noise of the excited Arena crowd could be plainly heard.

The glowing podiums began to rise, carrying the Gladiators up towards the Arena above. As they ascended, each fighter struck a commanding pose – chest puffed, chin high, feet planted wide.

Within seconds, they had disappeared from view. The sound of the crowd dropped in volume as the podiums plugged the ceiling holes. Even so, the cadets could still hear the enthusiastic yells, screams and applause that greeted the arrival of the Gladiators.

Rake listened to the excited cheering.

They wouldn't be so impressed if they knew the whole thing was a sham.

Before his enrolment as an Armouron knight, Rake's ambition had been to become the most famous Gladiator the Arena had ever seen. Now he knew that the Gladiators' celebrity was built on a lie. Their fights were fixed.

From here on in, although he still wanted to win every Gladiator medallion he could for competition and achievement, he was going to fight for more than a phoney trophy. He would fight for the Armouron ideals: Honour,

Duty, Compassion and Justice. And maybe one day, the people of Nu-Topia would chant *his* name, as they were now chanting Stamper's . . .

A dig in the ribs from Hoax put a stop to Rake's daydreaming.

'Come on, let's get somewhere we can watch!'

The other attendants were now making their way out of the chamber's main exit. Rake and Hoax quietly headed for a second, smaller passageway. As they did so, they were joined by another cadet – a girl, younger than either of them, with a slight build and striking white hair.

'Hiya, Snow,' whispered Hoax. 'Coming to see the show?'

The girl nodded silently.

'Count me in too!'

All three cadets started at the sound of a voice right behind them. A tanned, wirily built girl of around Rake's age stepped out of the shadows near the chamber wall. Unlike the other three children, she wasn't wearing the standard white tunic of an Academy student.

'Tea-Leaf! What are you doing here?' hissed Rake. 'I thought you were supposed to stay down in the Old School!'

'Yeah, yeah,' said Tea-Leaf. 'But Salt has had me polishing shield studs for about a century now. *Soooo* boring! He's busy in his workshop, so I thought I'd sneak up and grab a front-row seat with you lot.' She dismissed Rake's frown. 'Don't worry! Nobody's seen me but you. Stealth is my thing, remember?' She struck an exaggerated pose and whispered dramatically, 'I'm Balista, the Shadow . . .'

Hoax and Snow grinned, but Rake looked unimpressed.

'I heard Stamper getting stroppy just now,' continued the newcomer. 'He really has got it in for you, hasn't he, Rake?'

'Er, not now, Tea-Leaf,' warned Hoax, sensing the rising flush in his best friend's cheeks.

But Tea-Leaf didn't take the hint.

'I mean, there's no way I'd let him talk to *me* like that.'

The anger that Rake had been bottling up now came flooding out. He confronted Tea-Leaf furiously.

'Is that right? So what would you have done, exactly?' His voice dropped to an angry whisper. 'Used your Armouron training to lay a few moves

🎟 ♈ ⬥ ⬤ 🉐 🅰 🜂 ◍ ◎ ⬡ ✵

on him, hmm? Or do you not think there's a teensy chance that doing that might have blown our cover, and that maybe that would have been a bit *stupid*?'

Tea-Leaf had touched a nerve. In truth, using his new skills to take down Stamper was exactly what Rake would have instinctively liked to do. But he was already developing a sense of the responsibility that came with his Armouron role. In joining the order, they had become part of a noble, timeless tradition. Its teachings weren't to be employed lightly, in the heat of a petty squabble.

Tea-Leaf looked taken aback.

'No . . . I didn't mean . . .'

'Good!' snapped Rake. 'Because Salt told us not to draw attention to ourselves, remember? Which is why right now you should be down in the Old School, or hanging out with your precious street-friends, instead of risking—'

'Time out, you two!' protested Hoax. 'If we don't get a move on, we'll miss the start. Come on!'